The Last Sakura

The Last Sakura
Tales of the Yuta

ASHLEY NAKANISHI

Lōʻihi Press
Honolulu

Illustrations and cover art by Toni Silva

Edited by Lydia Haff

Uchinaaguchi translations by Brandon A. Ufugusuku-Ing

Gyosho title font by João Paulo Evangelista

Lōʻihi Press
www.loihipress.com
735 Bishop Street, Suite 235
Honolulu, Hawaiʻi 96813

Preface

This book is in dedication to the perpetuation of Uchinaanchu stories, histories, and culture. I wrote this with the intention of educating our youth from 0-108 years old, be they "haafu" or full-blooded, about Okinawa—to learn more about our history, folklore, and language.

All of this started with my mother, Sato, and grandmother, Tomi, who told stories during Obon about our ancestors and loved ones who were no longer with us. From there, I was inspired to create a book that our future generations can relate and hold on to.

Joyce Chinen, former President and Director of the Center of Okinawan Studies at University of Hawai'i at Mānoa, encouraged me to use my writing to inspire Shimanchu youth to be proud of their rich culture and history.

Through Shoji Endo and his collection of stories in *Folk Tales of Okinawa,* I was able to gain much of the knowledge of local lore, in addition to my generous studies and research elsewhere.

The text is supported by the *Okinawan-English Dictionary* written by Mitsugu Sakihara and *Rikka, Uchinaa-nkai!* by Masashi Sakihara, Shigehisa Karimata, Moriyo Shimabukuro, Lucilla Etsuko Gibo, and Brandon A. Ufugusuku-Ing; with consultation from Lee Tonouchi, the master of Hawaiian Pidgin and fellow Uchinaanchu brother.

Finally, through all of these combined efforts, the stories you find within this book were inspired by family, friends, and research during my time working at the Center of Okinawan Studies and thereafter.

It is my sincerest hope, as you read *The Last Sakura* series, you are able to resonate with some of these stories or share them with your loved ones.

May you enjoy reading this novel as much as I enjoyed writing it!

For our children, may they find pieces of themselves in this book and feel their ancestors in their spirit. — Ashley Nakanishi

To all my family and friends who believed in me and to my dad who convinced me to look at his friend's Facebook post. —Toni Silva

Contents

I Didn't Mean to Kill Her   1

Death Is No Paradise, Even in Hawai'i   5

What the Water Gives Us (Kiko)   9

When it Rains, it Pours   13

The Quiet Ride Home (Kiko)   17

Home, Again   21

Saying Goodbye (Kiko)   29

Point of No Return   33

The Hawai'i of Japan   35

The Long Drive "Home"   37

Are We There Yet?   41

The Village is Watching   43

Letting the Dust Settle   49

Misery Without Company   53

Insomnia and Insanity   63

Alienation Creates Allies   71

Strange Happenings (Kiko)   75

The Awakening   79

The Guardian of Iriomote   91

Yamamayaa   103

Tales of The Yuta   107

The Journey Back   113

Wishing Upon the Stars (Kiko)   119

Dreams and Nightmares   123

The Obon Festival (Kiko)   131

Accepting the Facts   135

Sometimes the "Crazy Family" Is Yours (Kiko)   145

Awakening the Spirits (Kiko)   151

Groveling at the Graves   165

Ichishini—Between Life and Death (Kiko)   173

Ukui—Saying Goodbye   181

A Means to An End   189

The Last Sakura (Kiko)   195

Acknowledgments   199

Intro to Uchinaaguchi   201

I Didn't Mean to Kill Her

"My mom! Please, you have to help her!" Kiko wailed. "Please!" she pleaded, exhausted from head to toe. The surfer pulled her onto his bodyboard and then dove below.

All she could really remember was the feeling of something, someone, pulling her into the water… the burning sensation on her ankle as she frantically kicked… her thick, ebony curls blocking everything in sight.

When the grasp of the undertow let up, there was only momentary relief before it dragged her back into its depths like some kind of monster. It wouldn't let go. The water was alive, and Kiko's every move challenged this invisible enemy who attempted to thwart her escape. Each kick was met with a stronger pull, and the saltwater she was sucking in stung the insides of her nose with such sharp intensity that it made her eyes wince. She felt something like a set of fingernails claw along her body, leaving papercut-like sensations all over. This, coupled with the feeling of water tickling her nose hairs as it curled down her throat, mimicking the very waves she hoped to escape, made Kiko feel helpless as she watched the surface move further and further away.

Time slowed as she sunk deeper into the water. Kiko could withstand a good amount of depth because of the countless times she had gone freediving with her mother, and drowning had always seemed like one of those impossible things, but as with any contender who has met her match, a wave of acceptance rolled over her, caressing her like a consoling father.

She remembered reading somewhere that there is this indecipherable peace to death—that it can feel like returning back to the earth. But in this case, Kiko was returning back to the water.

Or so she thought. The water above split like a bolt of white lightning, followed by a muffled thunderclap. It was as if the ocean had been broken apart by Kanaloa himself. But it was her. Within a prism of light, Kiko could make out her mother's familiar coarse black hair coiling behind her, and her paddling hands fanned out like the wings of a manta ray as she approached with a particular beauty Kiko hadn't quite noticed before. Small bubbles gathered at the corners of her mouth, nose, and eyes, illuminating a faint scar, an old burn that stretched across her face, hairline to jaw. Equally frightened and relieved, a tunnel of air fled from Kiko's lips as she tried to scream, "Mom!"

Kiko felt her mother pulling with all of the might her petite frame could muster before finally swimming underneath and kicking her feet, pedaling Kiko's body back toward the surface. Kiko tried to help by summoning the last bit of energy she had, pushing against her mother to propel herself upward. She thought she heard her mom cry out in pain, but the frantic kicking of her feet made it impossible to see behind her, and even though Kiko wanted so desperately to swim back to her, it was as if her body and brain were disconnected.

She broke the surface with screams for help, but saw nobody that could hear her. So she inhaled as much breath as possible, steadied herself with courage, and dove back under. But her mother was gone. The deep blue sea masked all within its elusive darkness. "Mom!" Kiko screamed into the sky as she surfaced again, as if calling the gods to help her. "Please! Anyone! Please help!" she cried out before going under again, hoping someone out there could hear her.

Then in the distance, she finally saw a bodyboarder. She waved frantically, hoping to catch his attention, and she did. He made his way toward her, but his seemingly long arm strokes only reminded her how far away he was. It seemed that in situations like this, fast is never fast enough, and as he pressed on, Kiko could no longer keep her head above water. Her hands, grasping for the surface, only became tangled within her thick hair floating in the water like limu.

The pulling of her body came as a surprise, so much so that her first reaction was to elbow the bodyboarder in the face as he hauled her onto his board.

"Are you okay?" he yelled into her face the way fools yell at deaf people. "What the hell are you doing out here by yourself—"

"My mom!" Kiko wailed, pleading with him to find her.

He dove then returned, then dove again, each time asking if Kiko was sure her mom was there. *Where did she swim up? How far did she drift before he got to her?* She insisted he keep searching, but deep down, she knew her mother was gone.

The Honolulu Fire Department scoured the waters with their jet skis, boats, and stand-up paddle boards for hours. Local divers offered a hand and swam as deep as they could, but a body was nowhere to be found. Lost to the space-like abyss of the sea.

And this is where we begin.

Death Is No Paradise, Even in Hawai'i

Tutu, their hānai grandmother, invited everyone to the funeral service: the neighbors, her co-workers, the rescue teams who searched for Kiko's mother, the bodyboarder who found Kiko, and she even placed an open invitation in the *Sun Advertiser*.

Tutu was big-boned, of a wise stature, and often wore colorful mu'umu'u at large gatherings. Her arms, capable of both grace and strength, were banded with traditional gold bracelets and tattoos.

But hours before the service began, she was still wearing loose, light denim pants that cut off around her calves and a simple T-shirt that hid some of the weight she had gained over the years. Her broad face had an even broader smile, with teeth that shined brighter than plumeria petals, and eyes that were as dark and deep as the valley she came from in Kaua'i. Her white hair, adorned with yellow hibiscus flowers, perfectly matched the haku lei she made at the senior center. She was tough, always spoke her mind, and fed you real good after, so you could digest her words and swallow your pride with a loving meal. She was everyone's aunty or tutu, especially during hard times.

When Kiko thought of her, she remembered being houseless, and Tutu giving them a home. She remembered all the times her mom and Tutu would bicker like mother and daughter and all the times she went to pick them up from school or drop them off in the mornings when their mom had to leave early to work. Although they were not blood-related, she defined family as whoever you wanted it to be: the people who show up when it matters. So no matter how upset it made Kiko that she didn't recognize many people at the funeral, she knew Tutu did this out of her own heart and grief.

Death is an occasion to celebrate one's life journey in Hawai'i. And Tutu was their mom's party planner. It made Kiko think people just like being anywhere that means not being alone because everyone—news crews, the mayor, men in fancy military uniforms, famous local surfers, neighbors, co-workers, and even the houseless families she worked with—were there.

It was as though her mom was a famous movie star or something. The huge crowd of people paddled out into the sunset to pay their respects, where Diamond Head Crater stood tall against the sky and a bright coral reef of colors foamed at its mouth like salt.

When Kiko closed her eyes for too long, she could picture her mother's hand sinking into the water, ever so slowly. Even in death, she was graceful.

Looking up to the sky, Kiko could tell heavy rain was coming soon. The paddlers could too, and one-by-one, each made their way back to shore. Then a sudden choking sensation came over her. The tiny hairs in her nose burned with salt, tearing at her esophagus, the taste of it bitter and overwhelming. She curled into herself with a heavy, sinking pain, drawing attention from others nearby. When the rain fell, it pierced her skin as if she were dehydrated, and maybe she was, having cried all the water out of her body at this point.

When she finally looked up, she caught the final breath of the night's sunset. Its soft lavender and creamsicle colors melted into each other, as if to dull the brilliance of what little sunlight was left as it faded into the horizon.

Tutu says in Hawai'i, when it rains, blessings are upon us. Yet, when it rains, people always get upset. When they're swimming and it rains, they leave to avoid sharks, supposedly, or leave the trails because rain makes them dangerous. So Kiko was not sure why Tutu thought this. She said it every time the clouds turned gray, then headed outside to stand in it and "receive the blessings."

But for some reason, she didn't say that today, and now, it was all Kiko could think about. It made her mad at Tutu really, and she didn't know why. Maybe Tutu realized that today was no blessing. In fact, today felt cursed.

What the Water Gives Us (Kiko)

I realized I hadn't touched water since. Not even here. I wanted to paddle out when the surfers asked. I wanted to say yes. I had attempted going into the sea several times over the last couple weeks, but each time I felt the tide pull at my feet, or I closed my eyes in the water—even just the taste of salt in the air would trigger the memories, and I felt as if I was drowning all over again. Losing her all over again.

"Tita, it's okay fo' cry, you know," whispered Tutu. Her sun-spotted hand tightened around my own, as if to pull me out of my thoughts. Suddenly, that heavy feeling congested my chest again, and tears pooled at my eyes. I think I needed to hear someone tell me it was okay for me to cry too.

"Do they hate me? Do they think it's my fault too?" Somehow saying it aloud hurt even more. Tutu's face didn't seem to be anything but pitiful. I could tell she didn't know the words to say.

"No, Bebeh," she said warmly. "Dey jus' don't know what fo' say—cuz they know you hurtin'."

Quickly, I swallowed the knot in my throat, brushed away my tears, and pulled myself together.

"Tutu," Yuki said in a loud whisper. "Why do we have that, if they never found mommy's body?" Her small finger pointing at the casket, while her other hand made scarce efforts to hide her question.

It's true. They never did, I thought, as we circled her portrait.

The rain grew heavier and faster, soaking my face and masking my tears. Perhaps that's what she really meant by blessings. The downpour allowed me to cry for the first time since it all happened. The ugly kind of cry we don't like others to see.

The weakness I felt inside washed away because now everyone looked like they were ugly crying too. Their hands wiped at their eyes as they walked at a steady but welcoming pace, yet unable to meet one another's somber gaze.

Although I knew people were in tears, I couldn't hear them over my sister, Yuki, whose cries cut my eardrums like paper. I could feel the grip on Tutu's hands tighten in irritation, as she side-eyed Yuki. When her shrill cries began to interrupt the service, she finally took her to the side.

So there I was, stuck in the front row facing my mother's portrait—with everybody staring. It was her raven-black eyes that pierced my soul, and her thick, coarse curls occupying the whole of her shoulders. Aside from a few sunspots and the faint scar bridging her left brow and cheekbone, her beauty was unmatched.

In fact, it was all anyone could talk about as they approached the picture. It wasn't long before her portrait was covered with orchid, ti, and puakenikeni leis. She would have loved all the flowers. I remember at weddings and funerals, she would always be sure to snag some of the plants if others planned to throw them out afterwards. Or how she would ask random people during walks in our neighborhood if she could take their dying plants home to remedy, returning them once in bloom again. She was funny like that, and people loved it about her. Mom had what Tutu called a green thumb. It was magical the way she healed plants, people, anything really.

Do you ever hear "sorry" so much that it stops feeling real?

I never knew that feeling until then. When each person made it a point to tell me how sorry they were, I felt like they wanted to hear me say sorry too. To admit this was somehow my fault. It was the look in their eyes, silently pitying the girl who drowned her mother. Or maybe it was to make themselves feel better—pretending that we were going to be okay. But there was no avoiding the lingering sensation that nobody really wanted me there.

My attention was constantly divided between their apologies and watching my mother's face disappear all over again behind them.

I hear losing a parent or a child is like losing a piece of yourself. The piece others talk about "missing" when they bring you up in private conversations. I could hear people talking about me, asking Tutu if "she is alright" or how they noticed "her mana is in a dark place," as if I couldn't hear their countless questions or comments. Well, that's probably because I had my headphones on throughout the reception. It wasn't plugged into anything. I just learned this was the best way to ignore and be ignored by others. To say "back off" without having to be "one tita" about it, as Tutu would say.

They weren't wrong. I haven't felt the same. I felt angry now. All the time. Even today, especially today, as I see all these people eating and criticizing the food we stayed up all night preparing. Talking, smiling, and even laughing through our mother's funeral. A quiet rage filled my soul. It swallowed my body like water, forcing my eyes shut. The salt in my tears stuck to my eyelids like wallpaper, and all I could see was her hand, floating in the water. And then me not being strong enough to help her. Not being strong enough to help myself.

I felt like the funeral wasn't really for us as much as it was about keeping everyone else happy, their bellies full, and leaving enough time for the aunties and uncles to swap gossip with Tutu them, while all the older cousins babysat the keiki running around Kapiʻolani Park. All the others seemed to compliment Yuki on her dancing and her finely pressed floral dress. Yuki, of course, ate up the compliments and spent most of her time playing with the other kids, while I sat on a bench under one of the large banyan trees, away from everyone.

Their energies were too much. I could feel what everyone was feeling, and I just wanted to be by myself, in my own thoughts. Mom always called me empathic. "A superpower which runs in our family," she would say to make me feel better. "A blessing and a curse." I could sense that she had it too. I loved these old banyan trees though. Mom said they were portals between the dead and living —which was particularly comforting today.

Finally, everyone in our hānai family started to pack up and say their goodbyes. Have you ever felt eyes on your skin? That sounds weird. What I mean is have you ever felt eyes following you wherever you went? Well, I couldn't help but feel like someone was watching us. Me.

I took off my headphones and looked around, before noticing a man in full uniform standing off to the side, lurking between the sidewalk and trees like a creeper. He wore this confused look on his face, like a lost dog. At first glance, I thought it was our father: the long navy-blue slacks with red bands running down the hems, the thick, black coat with golden buttons pinned against his chest, wrists, and pockets, the thick, white belt with a shiny square buckle, and his head topped with a pearly-white military cap that had an emblem of the world wrapped in rope. Just how I remembered him from the pictures.

"Do you know that guy?" asked Yuki.

I suddenly realized I wasn't alone. "I don't know—kinda looks like dad," I said. "Wait here."

"Dad? Like our dad?" Yuki asked, her face contorted with excitement.

"Just—" I tried to find a way to be nice, but my mind was scrambling for answers too. "Wait here."

I walked toward him. He noticed and met my pace until we found ourselves only feet away from each other. Suddenly, there was this feeling telling me I didn't know this person. He looked much younger than the guy in the photos our mom always showed us. I stopped dead in my tracks and mustered an amount of bravery I didn't actually have, I shouted, "Hey! Who are you looking for?" in my deepest voice.

He took off his cap, gently placing it under his right arm. His hair was blonde and faded, and his face was pale and freckled, with light eyes that pierced your skin with a lonely stare. His body language was distant and robotic, like most military guys we see on Oʻahu. My heart began to race as he slowly walked over, and then stopped when he was only steps away.

When it Rains, it Pours

The man stood confidently before Kiko, but she could tell he was nervous. She felt it in her bones. Her stomach turned and twisted, unsure if she could handle any more emotional turbulence today.

He studied her face, seeming to understand. His posture relaxed, and he knelt down on one knee, dirtying his dress blues to bring himself down to her short, rotund stature.

"Ma'am, I apologize," he said with a thick Southern accent. "I'm looking for a... a Kee-ko and um... a... a Yucky? I may not be sayin' it right but... uh... you know who I'm talkin' about? I think they're around your age, but all I have is this picture and it ain't really helping much." Kiko couldn't tell what kind of Southern accent he had, but it sounded familiar. "In fact, I've been all over the park this afternoon hoping to find these girls and been yelled at by I can't tell you how many people, but I figured with a gathering this big I must be at the right..." Giving up, he held out the aged and worn photo. "Could you tell me if you recognize this man here," he said, pointing at a tall, white man with penetrating, mismatched eyes. Next to him, attempting to stand with her young legs between her mother and her father who was holding Yuki in his arms, was Kiko in what seemed like the perfect family photo in front of Shuri Castle in Okinawa.

"You mean Kiko and Yuki?" she said, being sure to show him how to say their names correctly, something her mother often insisted when speaking with "gaijin, haoles, or teachers who think names don't matter."

"And who are you exactly?" Kiko snarled.

"I apologize, ma'am. Staff Sergeant Jackson. I'm with the United States Marine Corp. I was sent to deliver this uh... a letter and flowers for the... um... deceased relations of one our fellow servicemen."

In his hand was a white envelope. She had seen them before at funerals, a common Japanese practice—even here in Hawai'i. It was slender, with Japanese calligraphy running down the center and a black and white ribbon knotted like an eternity sign down the middle.

They tend to say things along the lines of "my deepest condolences," whatever that meant, Kiko thought. More so, she just remembered it often included money to help pay for the funeral when "sorry" wasn't enough.

Instantly, Kiko felt her face and ears burning; her heart was racing all over again. Here was this envelope with money, but no father in sight. This was not unusual. Their mother remarked to Tutu one time that, "His money was more valuable than his presence ever could be."

But never did she accept it—she always tore up his checks or threw his letters away. So, to follow the same suit, Kiko pushed the envelope back.

"So where is he, huh?" she growled. "This mystery father. Seems like an asshole to me. Most fathers would be at their kids' mother's funeral, don't you think?"

"Uh..." Jackson began to sweat. He cleared his throat and pushed on to say, "He is at his station in Okinawa, ma'am. I assume by the look on your face you must be..." He paused to look down at his paper. "Kiko, I assume? Am I sayin' that right?" he asked, pointing to the toddler in the picture.

"Depends." Kiko bit into the air, wanting him to know she wasn't playing games. "Just tell me what you want! If you didn't notice, we're busy."

"Right, of course." He hesitantly pulled out another envelope tucked under his arm. "Here," he said softly. "There you are, ma'am."

"So, why isn't he here? Did he at least tell you that?" Kiko demanded.

"Honestly ma'am, I don't know the man at all—not really my department. But I am sure it's all there in the letter. Again, my condolences, ma'am."

"Stop calling me ma'am! It's Kiko!" she shouted, making a turn-key gesture. "Like a key and koh! Key-koh! Kiko dammit!"

"I apologize, Ki... Kiko. My condolences about your mama. I ain't never lost my mama, but I know you must be in a whirlwind of pain. I'll be on my way. Again, my apologies," Jackson said, his cheeks flush with shame, or maybe guilt.

"Why? Did you kill her?" Kiko asked bluntly and dead-faced. He looked terrified. "Then don't apologize. I'm sick of hearing everyone tell me how 'sorry' they are. You didn't even know her."

He quickly and quietly put the envelopes back into the folder and handed her both, as well as a bouquet of white lilies—flowers she didn't even like. It made her wonder if their father knew her at all, if he even cared. Why wouldn't he show up himself? Where was he? How was the woman who gave us life not worth being here for? I hate him, Kiko thought. He is weak. He is nothing. He is not worth your attention, Kiko. He is not worth these tears!

Thoughts like this rushed to Kiko's mind like pooling water and she felt like she was drowning in her emotions as she walked back to Yuki, who had been watching the whole scene with Jackson the way animals look at people in the zoo. She didn't say anything as Kiko came to her. She knew better than that. Instead, she just held out her hand, Kiko took it, and they returned to the procession, somber but together.

The Quiet Ride Home
(Kiko)

The ride home wasn't quite like the movies when the main character's mother dies. Tutu was "talkin' story" about all the people she saw at the funeral—who she liked, didn't like, the ones she "nevah know why was dea," and what food we shoulda had because now "everybody prolly stay hungry and talkin' stink 'bout us." I think she was mostly trying to distract Yuki, who was always somewhere between crying and laughing. I found her happiness to be as annoying as it was offensive. Since the Pali was closed down due to a landslide, we were forced to take the scenic route home from Waikiki.

"So, you goin' tell me what da haole wen' say to you or what?" Tutu asked impatiently. Her thin brow raised like a hill in the rearview mirror. It was her way of saying, "tell me what I wanna know." But I didn't care to talk.

"They were talking forever!" shouted Yuki.

"Dat right? 'Bout what? He nevah say nothing?"

"No—" I began to say.

"No?" Yuki asked. "So you just stood there? He handed you something! I seen it! Tutu, I seen it!"

"No!" I yelled. "Ugh! Let me finish! He said, 'My condolences' over and over, then he gave me this letter from our dad. You weren't even there, Yuki, so shut up already!"

"Eh—no ack! Tell ya sistah sorry!" barked Tutu. "No reason fo' tell her shaddap when you no like say nothing!"

"Ugh. Whatev—"

Before I could even finish, Tutu's hand flew through the air and swatted me in the face. "No 'whateva' me, Tita. I know you in one bad place, but this not how we ack. You say sorry to ya sistah, now!" She waited only moments before snapping another three syllables at me: "What? Like slaps?"

"Sorry, *Princess* Yuki," I spat out, and Yuki sneered back in victory.

Yuki was a spoiled brat, and it was because she was the baby. She always got what she wanted. All she had to do was shed a couple tears and sniffle, and everyone would drop everything to make her smile.

Then, as if by some miracle, everyone finally stopped talking. Silence filled the car again, until Tutu began to sing along with Braddah Iz's "Somewhere Over the Rainbow," as it played on the radio. When the song came to an end, it was like she couldn't help it; she had to ask, "So... What did ya faddah say?"

"I don't know," I responded. "I haven't read it yet. I don't really care, to be honest."

"I can read it! I read better than you anyway!" blared Yuki, finally looking up from her drawing pad.

I felt anger course through my veins like lightning, leaving a burning feeling in my chest. Of course, she would say that and get away with it. It was as if I couldn't even help what happened next. I snatched her drawing pad and yelled, "It's like you don't even care! All you want to do is open things! All you care about are presents! Our mom is dead! And all you can do is draw, draw, draw!"

Yuki's eyes welled with tears, clinging to her lashes and falling down her face like the rain falling outside over Hawai'i Kai. Her single, thick eyebrow furrowed in the center, and I could see all the blood rush to her face and into the corners of her lips as she gathered enough breath to send out a blood-curdling, "Give it back!"

Tutu's hand swatted back and forth, reaching behind and swinging like a wrecking ball until she connected with my face again. "What in da *hell* is wrong with you, Kiko? Ack'n laddaht! Give it back. Now!"

"Whatever," I said, "take your stupid book." I tossed the unicorn drawing pad to Yuki's side of the car, then used my hands to gather cold fog from the window to press against the itching, burning sensation that Tutu left across my cheek. I was so mad, the tears felt hot as they steamrolled down my chin and onto the envelope in my lap. I could feel Tutu's guilt emanating from the front seat.

"Eh, Tita. I know you hurting, and I no like fo' lick you but—" Tutu said before jerking the car to the side and honking at a purple

Jeep that cut into our lane. As if making a complete 180° spiritually, she rolled down her window yelling, "Fakah learn fo' drive! Use ya blinkah, frickin donkey!" She swerved into the next lane while she stuck finger outside the window and honked over and over again. "These frickin tourists, brah! Dey tink dey own da whole frickin road!"

I couldn't help but smirk a little. Tutu was always so funny when we drove. She always insisted on driving, but then would complain the entire time about other drivers or having to drive anywhere. But in times like this, Yuki and I would look at each other and smile while Tutu used all the words she gave us lickings for. But it wasn't long before we remembered we were still mad at each other, and the car slipped back into a muffled static.

So, I plugged in my headphones and decided to tune out.

Yuki returned to her drawing for a while before falling asleep and Tutu was singing quietly and drove, wiping tears from her face every once in a while, looking back in the rearview mirror, making sure we didn't catch her crying either. I didn't have to look up to know; I could feel her pain radiate like a pulse. Blessing and a curse, right?

Honestly, I forgot how pretty Koko Head looked at night with the stars all glittering around its peak.

I stared out into the neighborhood that led to a secret lava site we went to every once in a while. It was the only place on the island where we could see all the stars and the city streetlights at the same time.

I remembered how we would go and watch the cave-like lava tubes spit out water the way whales do. Our mom often stared into the sky and listened to the waves crash into the caves and sea walls, as they stretched across the smooth and ancient lava flows, like the star sand she brought home from Okinawa long ago.

I loved hearing the story of how the stars were the bodies of gods who fell from the sky, that Okinawa was the only place in the world where it existed. Only then, I couldn't remember how it went, and trying to remember only pushed the memory further away. It was the kind of pain that broke my heart because I felt like I was already beginning to forget her. Somewhere between choking back tears and the exhaustion of that day, I tried my best to sleep the pain away.

Home, Again

Kiko woke as the engine shut off in front of their house in Enchanted Lake. It looked the same, but different. She thought maybe it was the way the light from the moon turned the house into different colors. The white had cooled into a deep blue, the green trimmings into a cold black. The yellow French doors were dull and deep mustard now.

But the garden, her mother's garden, full of local and native Hawaiian plants, huge elephant ears, crawling ferns, Okinawan sweet potato vines, tomatoes, green beans, bittermelon, shampoo ginger, and large birds of paradise that seemed to look particularly bright and stood out more than ever.

Tutu lived in the upstairs unit of their single-story cottage, above the garage. She used to live downstairs when her husband was alive, but couldn't bring herself to stay in the house long ever since he'd died at sea, and she preferred to stay upstairs whenever possible. However, it was because of this that their mom could even get the house because most people didn't rent to single mothers.

Especially single, immigrant mothers with two young children. Tutu must have convinced herself it was a good way to make a steady income, but she knew the loneliness and grief coupled with the memories of first moving into the home were the real reasons she took them in. They had lived there ever since. If anyone ever asked, she wouldn't be able to tell you what life was like before they arrived, and the girls wouldn't be able to tell you about a life without Tutu in it.

Kiko could only faintly do so, remembering only the small mango tree that existed when they first moved in. She always wondered if all the effort she put into the house and garden was her mom's way of paying Tutu back—with the literal fruits of her labor.

"You hungry, bebeh?" Tutu asked, interrupting Kiko's train of thought.

"No, thank you," she said quietly, still staring at the house.

Tutu smiled. "Tutu gon' make you sum'ting anyway."

"I said I'm not hungry."

"I know, I know. So I gon' make em' anyway. Can eat em' bumbai." She turned away and opened the door to get Yuki.

Even though Tutu seemed ancient to Kiko, she could always muster the strength to pick up their drowsy, boneless bodies from the car whenever they fell asleep. Even though Yuki was eight years old now and nearly stood at Tutu's chest, she still managed to throw Yuki over her shoulder and carry her up the stairs to her garage studio without waking her. But it looked to be getting harder year by year, especially as she was having a hard time getting herself up the stairs these days too.

"Tutu, can I grab something from inside our house really fast?" Kiko asked, knowing the inconvenience of timing would likely work in her favor.

"Yeah, bebeh," she gasped. "Da keys stay upstairs. Try hurreh and open da door for me too. This chick, so heavy already!"

"Yes, Tutu." Kiko squeezed between her, Yuki, and the wall, moving upstairs as quickly as possible.

"And Kiko—Hurreh up, ah? No dakine, dilly dally. I stay organizing all your guys' tings and no like you mess em' up."

Tutu wasn't kidding. The inside looked different. There were boxes everywhere. Some stacked on top of each other. Others taped-up and piled by the door marked GOODWILL, BOOKS, STORAGE, and FRAGILE. A few were left unmarked, open with only a few items inside such as blankets, photos, and things from her butsudan left inside. It had been only a couple weeks, and it felt to Kiko as if they were being erased from its walls. It was the first time she wondered where they would go from here.

The house was colder than usual, and Kiko could have sworn she heard a slight swishing of feet on the tatami mats as if someone walked inside, so she ran to turn on the lights in the rest of the house. Of course, it was nothing but a huge Io moth, resting on the mantle inside. A chill ran down her spine and made her feel otherwise. She felt something there; she just didn't know what.

Although she wanted to believe she wasn't scared of things like ghosts, she quickly walked to her room which was left unchanged. It wasn't glamorous, as Kiko was known to be a bit of a slob, with drawings and achievement certificates hanging on the walls, and a desk still messy from the projects she started and never finished. But what she wanted now more than ever was the bed she had complained about for months leading up to now, which suddenly seemed more attractive than ever to her young, bone-weary body.

Out the corner of her eye, she couldn't help but notice the last stack of laundry her mother had placed neatly on the white three-drawer dresser next to her bed. She picked up the purple Okinawan Festival T-shirt her mom got last year and pajamas from the top of the stack and held them close to her face. Doing her best to mute her tears, it wouldn't be long before Kiko began cry-screaming into her garments, hoping to muffle her agony. Nobody could make clothes smell the way she did. If the sun had a smell, it was this. It felt like her mom was here again, if only for a moment. Kiko's eyes shifted to each corner of the room, hoping to catch shadows in her peripheral vision.

Finally, sitting on the edge of her bed, she slowly put on her mother's gently folded clothes. In doing so, the small worn out Polaroid of her family fell out of her pocket. At once, she remembered the procession, First Sergeant Jackass, and the envelopes from her father. Her body folded over like a fern as she breathed deeply, feeling her lungs pushing against her ribs, and exhaled with a sense that change was coming.

"Kiko!" Tutu yelled. "Get ya okole up hea! Didn't I say hurreh ahp? It's late—come eat!"

"Coming, Tutu!" Kiko shouted back, using her hands to amplify her words.

She quickly turned off the lights and locked up, making sure to go back to the car and retrieve the envelope. Kiko couldn't tell if it was all the romantic comedics her mom watched or all the Shakespeare tragedies and books she grew up reading, but one thing was for sure— letters were always a sign of bad news.

She trudged up the stairs, each breath more reluctant than the next. At the top, she slipped the envelope in her shirt, hoping to hide it from Tutu.

To no surprise, there was a huge feast prepared in the short time Kiko was downstairs. She could smell it downwind as she entered from the stairwell, and with the creepy vibes she was getting from downstairs, she made sure to lock the door behind her. After taking off her shoes, she stepped into the dining area and sat at the small table littered with newspaper and coupon clippings, assorted goods, and Tutu's glasses and magnifying glass.

Kiko took out her letter, put it out on the table then put it back into her shirt, unable to think of a better place to hide it. Tutu's house was just like her—an organized kind of chaos. But her heart, her soul, was in the kitchen, a treasure trove of hanging plants, spices, herbs, and books that crowded her counter-tops. Tutu was almost always in the kitchen. Or in her room watching Korean soap operas.

She stood over the stovetop in her night muʻumuʻu, a well-worn black dress with sun-beaten yellow hibiscuses that trailed into its lightly tethered ends. On each burner was a different pot or pan, filled with lau lau, rice, poi, or Chinese long rice—leftovers from the funeral.

Without warning, Kiko was brimming with an insatiable hunger, water filling her mouth and her stomach growling with such ferocity she may as well have been the beast that boys at school teased her about being, pointing at her hairy legs and arms.

"See," Tutu said with a smirk. "Wen' tell you. I knew you was gon' get hungry. Well, hurreh ahp. Get em' while it's hot. Oh—mind cleaning off the table too? Tanks, Bebeh."

Kiko tried to remain as indifferent as possible because quite frankly, she hated when Tutu was right, but her body was in survival mode, and mechanically, she appeared at the stove making a plate. The speed with which Kiko made it from the stove to the table, and how fast the food moved from the plate to her mouth, proved that Tutu was right and Kiko was wrong. They exchanged a silent agreement that only eyes can. Her bloated belly started pushing the envelope further up her shirt, protruding like the ribs of some kind of werewolf amid its transformation.

"Tita," Tutu said affectionately, nodding her head upward. "What's in ya shirt?"

"Um... nothing. My body?" Kiko muttered, defeated. How stupid to hide it there, she thought, hoping Tutu would just drop it and let her eat in peace.

She giggled and smiled with a large raised eyebrow, in that "you better say something" kind of way. "Oh yeah? It's one full moon tonight, right? What, you turning into—one wolf?" Tutu half-shouted in laughter, struggling to get the last words out of her mouth.

Kiko looked down and realized how foolish she appeared and even though she didn't want to laugh, the edges of her lips curled. "I was just thinking that too." She smiled, comforted by their connection.

"It's the letter... from our dad."

"Well yeah, duh, not gon' take Sherlock Holmes fo' figure dat one out. You gon' read em? It won't open itself, you know."

As if by magic, Yuki burst out of her slumber and appeared in the kitchen, stretching side to side by the stovetop, making a plate herself.

"I can open it," she yawned as if trying to mask her excitement. "I love opening stuff."

"We all know that, Yuki. But this isn't a present," Kiko uttered under her breath, annoyed.

"She's right, Yuki. That's her kuleana for open em. Go on. I can help you read if need be."

Hesitating, Kiko delicately unfolded the eternity knot, setting it to the side the way mom taught them to when it came to letters or even fancy wrapping paper. Her fingers began to shake, as her forefinger slid into the slit of the envelope.

Expecting money to fall out, she was surprised to see two JAL tickets take its traditional place. Behind the tickets were words scribbled into the card but they were all jumbled up to her, and his handwriting didn't really help. Kiko hated reading. She hated it when people watched her read. But she especially hated that his letter was so long and she was being put on the spot.

"Dear... Dearest Kiko and Yuki, I am sorry to... ear..." she fumbled.

"Hear," Tutu gently corrected her.

"I am sorry to hear of your mother's pa...as...passing. You grills..." Kiko stopped briefly, clearing her throat to buy time. "...girls. You girls will be—"

Yuki snatched the letter from her hands, quickly picking up where Kiko left off. "You girls will be leaving in two days to join me in Okinawa," Yuki nearly shouted as she ran away from Kiko into the living room, stopping to read when she could. "You will be staying with your grandmother, Tomi, until I can make further arrangements. She likes to be called Kachan. Remember her? I hope so. Please ask for ...ass... as... sis... tance from family to get your things in order. See you soon. Major General Shackles," Yuki blurted, catching her breath from reading it as fast as she had.

"Girl! What I wen' tell you!" Tutu scolded Yuki, snatching the letter from her hands and giving it back to Kiko. "Brrrrah! I asked her to read."

"I know, I know! But... but she can't even read! I'm eight and I can read better than her!"

"It's called dyslexia, stupid!" Kiko yelled back.

"Well, at least I don't sound stupid, stupid!" Yuki snarled.

"Eh—both you ack'n frickin' stupid! Kiko, try let me see the letter," Tutu said, her fingers rolling toward her palms like short, impatient waves breaking against rock.

She read over the letter and tickets, looking surprised more and more each time, swearing and cursing under her breath about how, "he gon' get bad bachi' for this!" Tutu threw it onto the table. "Girls brush ya teeth and go sleep already. I gon' call your faddah. You two get some rest."

"Ugh!" Kiko grunted. "I hate him!" She slammed her fists to the table, and then noticing the startled look on both of their faces, she apologized and excused herself to go to the bathroom.

There, from the slightly open door, she could just hear Yuki whisper, "Why is she always so angry?"

"No need be scared, Bebeh," Tutu said softly. "She jus' hurting. Let her hurt. And you, you eat. Still get that mac nut pie you like in the fridge. Den go brush ya teeth and go sleep. Kay?"

Later, Kiko couldn't sleep very well because she could hear Tutu outside on the phone, moving around late into the night.

By morning, the sweet aroma of breakfast drew her weary bones out of bed. She could tell bad news awaited them when she noticed the table was clear of Tutu's stuff and replaced with macadamia nut pancakes, fresh mangoes, dragonfruit, Spam, rice, eggs and steamed ulu with coconut milk. Quickly, she opened the fridge and was excited to see POG juice on the bottom shelf. But her feelings were right: in the corner of her drowsy eyes, she saw two suitcases, seemingly packed, lined up neatly by the front door. A sinking feeling came over her. "What's going on? Are we going somewhere?" But she knew the answer. She had seen the tickets.

"Ya faddah... he's one donkey," Tutu seethed. "Dummeh wen' grab da plane tickets for today, not next week. He nevah tink to include da time fo' da mail fo' get hea." She started pointing at her head. "So dramas! I had fo' pack everyting fo' you two last night. Not dat I could sleep anyway. I was so irrahz, trying fo' gather all dakine tings. Anyway, da plane leaves tonight, so I figure we'll throw da bags in da car and do whateva ya like until den. Maybe see Unko La'akea, whatchu tink?"

Kiko's chest hurt. Everything hurt. She didn't know how to respond, really. We were leaving? Already? What if Tutu didn't pack all the things she needed? What about school? Their friends?

"Ooooo! POG! My favorite!" Yuki squealed and she chugged two small cups of the passion orange guava juice she loved. "So what's the special occasion?" she asked, all wide-eyed and bushy-tailed.

"We're leaving. Forever. Today," Kiko replied plainly, hardly believing the words as they fled her mouth. "So think about what you wanna do before we go."

"We're leaving? O-M-G! That means I won't get Ms. Lee for third grade, right? Yasss! And we get to see our dad?"

"Yay," Kiko snipped sarcastically, idly waving her hands in the air before walking away.

Saying Goodbye
(Kiko)

We did all the typical stuff everyone does before leaving the island. We drove through the Eastside, down the windy roads of Kahalu'u, stopping at Kualoa to feed the horses and off to the shrimp trucks to eat. When we stopped by Ted's Bakery to snack on something sweet, Yuki grabbed the ube half-moon, while I grabbed my favorite, onolicious guava cream pie, which I ended up having to share anyway, before making our way toward Waimea rock to cruise em for the rest of the day.

I used to love jumping from the big rock, but I just couldn't. Honestly, I didn't know if I'd ever go in the ocean again. Tutu must have felt bad because we ended up leaving almost immediately to go across the street to Waimea Falls where Mom used to volunteer. Not really sure this was the best alternative, but since Yuki was happy, it was whatever.

Mom was here all the time, giving advice to others on how to take care of their plants or listing the health and other benefits of various botanicals. In fact, people would revisit the site specifically asking for her and talk stories forever! Like I said before, she was like a celebrity —even at the botanical gardens. Everyone loved her.

When we parked, I felt like crying or throwing up, perhaps both. Yuki couldn't get out of her seat fast enough, running straight to the cafe where La'akea (a guy who liked my mom a lot) was working. By the time Tutu and I made it up the stairs and past the solemn looks of Mom's co-workers, some of them offering apologies, we found Yuki already walking away from the counter, digging into her rainbow shave ice, slathered in condensed milk.

"Hey, Aunty Bobbi—how you?" La'akea asked, leaning in to kiss her cheek.

Tutu sighed heavily. "I good, Boo—how you doing?"

"Well, you know," he quietly responded, looking at me and Yuki and trying to remain level-headed. He came around the counter to greet Tutu properly, joining foreheads and exchanging their breaths. La'akea was tall and built like a warrior with tattoos that crawled up his arms and down his legs: tribal markings that detailed his family's legacy.

"Eh, you get nuff time to take the girls around today?" Tutu asked, sounding a little tired from being up so late.

Man, I loved La'akea. I was probably going to miss him the most. He was always letting me cook whatever I wanted and gave us the good snacks when we came to visit. He told the best stories and could make our mom laugh harder than anyone I'd ever known. Her smile never glowed that way with anyone else either, but she always denied anything romantic between them.

But today, he didn't look the same. It was like his light was fading. He didn't shine the same way he normally did, and when he hugged us, it was longer than usual. I could hear him inhale sharp breaths before he jumped up and started smiling as if nothing had happened.

"Shoots! I heard it's ya guys' last day! So how bout we take the cart up to the waterfalls and go cool off. Kiko, they get the life jackets if you like go in."

"No worries. I just wanna get some plants to make bookmarks if that's okay."

"Of course, boo. Just keep em between us though, ah? K den, let's get you one shave ice too and we go."

"I'm okay, uncle. Thank you."

"You sure?" His brows raised like he was shocked at my answer.

"Yeah, maybe when we get back. We had a big breakfast."

"Shoots. Aunty, you like anything?"

"No, boy, you jus' take da girls. I gon' relax in da shop. Get A.C.!" Tutu exclaimed, letting out a deep laugh and waving us off.

It was always fun to go in the cart, driving past all the haoles who looked like they were having heat strokes, as we sat with our battery-powered misting fans. It always made me feel like we were VIPs or something.

We stopped here and there to sneak small samples of fallen leaves, then rain began to drizzle about half-way up the trail, and as the breeze picked up, I could feel her everywhere. For the first time since that day, I felt like I could breathe again. I collected a few different orchids, puakenikeni, and a few sprigs from the 'ōhi'a lehua before we made our way to the waterfall where La'akea and Yuki swam, playing and splashing under the crashing spring water.

"I'm going to miss you, Uncle! Will you visit us?" Yuki asked on the way back down.

"Well, no. But I gon' try to work something out to where maybe we can pitch in for a ticket, so you guys can visit us during breaks—how does that sound?"

"Okay..." Yuki said with sad hopefulness, but she knew he didn't mean it. He knew he didn't mean it. I knew he didn't either, but none of us were willing to be honest with ourselves. All of a sudden us leaving felt really real. The rain came down, clapping against the asphalt like a standing ovation. What perfect timing, I thought, as tears rolled down my face. "Let the blessings begin," I muttered sarcastically, loud enough for La'akea to hear.

Tutu didn't realize there was going to be so much construction on the old roads back, so because she had already packed our luggage we headed straight to the airport, barely giving us time to give her a proper goodbye.

As we checked in, Yuki and I were sent to the counter to be "accompanied" by a thin Japanese flight attendant, who wore a black skirt with shiny black stockings, a fitted jacket with pretty red trimmings, and a scarf around her neck. Something about the look in her eyes said she wasn't very fond of children.

We held hands through the airport, and I couldn't help but think about all the stuff I hoped Tutu had packed and all the things we must have forgotten in rushing. If mom was here, we would have never had to rush—we would have been here hours ago. Tutu used to joke that "Japanee' hate to be late," to which my mom would give mean stink eye.

"Yeah, yeah I know—you's Okinawan, not Japanee, whateva."

"Not whatever. Two different cultures, language, and histories, Bobbi," she'd say, standing tall and proud. "Besides, there is nothing wrong with being punctual. Not everyone can run on Hawaiian time, you know."

Personally, I think she just liked to be in control of situations, and when she was early, she could do that—always playing host, even at other people's houses.

I could have sworn I had never been to an airport before, but obviously, we ended up in Hawai'i, and I remember bits and pieces of back then, but not here, not now. It looked like a mall! And it was priced like one too. But no matter whatever else Tutu might have neglected to pack, I was sure that she had packed us something to eat.

Point of No Return

The plane was crowded. It was a red-eye, and tourists and visiting families all had places to be, jobs and lives to get back to. The vacation was over for most of those on board, but Kiko and Yuki weren't sure what to feel.

They were allowed to go on first since they were "unaccompanied minors," and their seats were in the furthest row against the wall where the bathrooms and service stations were. "Basically, we're going to smell the food and people poop at the same time. Great." Kiko huffed. She helped Yuki get settled in, pulling out her tablet and setting up her snacks and drawing materials. All Kiko needed was her phone and headphones. Yuki was excited to see they had their own TV on the back of each seat and could watch whatever they wanted, but Kiko simply chose to watch the flight path crawl at a glacial pace across the Pacific. And with each little blip forward of the cartoon plane, she sunk further into the feeling of being at the point of no return, until, finally, she fell asleep.

Soon she was dreaming, drowning again, feeling her feet pushing down on her mother's shoulders, trying to stay up long enough to catch her breath before being pulled back under. Forcing herself to look around, she saw the faintest shadow of another figure beneath, above, and around them. Longer than an oarfish. Larger than a shark. It looked like something straight out of the Hawaiian legends Laʻakea used to talk about. She saw her mother's long hair gracefully veiling her face like a sea anemone, and out of the bubbles escaping her lips exploded pockets of screams, each one echoing louder than the next.

She saw the shadow of the surfer moving closer and fought with each kick, each stroke to reach the heavens above. To beg God to save them.

"Help!" Kiko cried out in pain. "Please help her!"

Breathing heavily, she shot wide awake, seeing people all around staring at her. Frightened, she couldn't hold back tears, but within minutes the people returned to their seats, their lives, their own problems, and the girls returned to the quiet stirring between them.

"Was it the dream again?" Yuki asked gently, offering her hand in reassurance.

With tears rolling down her face, Kiko clenched her jaw, biting at her own vulnerability and weakness. "No," she said, her body still quivering. "It's nothing."

The Hawai'i of Japan

"Ladies and Gentleman, welcome to Okinawa and Naha International Airport. We ask you to please remain seated with seatbelts on until we arrive at the gate," the captain called out in near-perfect English.

Kiko and Yuki stretched and cleaned up their areas, packing away their electronics and art supplies. The flight attendant helped them fill out a small paper form detailing their stay. "Your father should be waiting by the gate. You must be so excited, yes?"

"I am!" Yuki cheered.

Once free from the blistering heat of the jetway, they arrived downstairs in the terminal to find a tall, young white man in uniform holding a sign with the word "SHACKLES" scribbled in blurry neon ink.

"Wow. He couldn't even bother picking us up…" Kiko murmured under her breath.

"Do you think we get to go in a limousine?" Yuki asked excitedly.

To their grave disappointment, there was no limousine. In its place was an old Honda Civic. When the man threw their luggage inside, not so gently, Yuki's grip on Kiko's hand got tighter.

"You'll be okay," he said and motioned for them to get inside.

Kiko felt fear emanating off Yuki as they got into the car and drove away. In the rearview mirror, the man's cold, empty blue eyes looked back at them. She couldn't tell if he was curious or if he pitied them. "So, you gonna tell us where our dad is or what?" she asked bluntly.

"Yeah… and who are you?" Yuki asked in her bravest voice.

He chuckled. "My name is Jackson, David Jackson. I will be bringing you both to your father. Well, he is indisposed at the moment, but—"

"Jesus, is everyone's last name Jackson?" Kiko asked.

Jackson straightened his posture. "Excuse me, ma'am?"

"Nothing. Never mind."

"Okay... Well!" he exclaimed, as if attempting to change the mood. "I hear Okinawa is the Hawai'i of Japan. Never been there myself, but I hear it's just as beautiful! That's where y'all from right?"

"Right. Except that it isn't Hawai'i. You'd know that if *y'all* been there." Kiko plugged in her headphones and stared into the distance, ignoring everything and everyone.

The Long Drive "Home"

It was hot, musty, and nearly unbearable in the back of the car, as the marine tried to crank up his useless A.C. and play Smashing Pumpkin's greatest hits. Yuki insisted they split the headphones between the two of them, and they struggled to listen to a few songs on Yuki's iPad on repeat as they drove along the Miyakojima Highway, taking in the breathtaking views of the pristine waters full of rich coral reef and islands like skipping stones across the sand and shore.

As usual, Yuki fell asleep within the first hour of driving and conversations became rather minimal in the car. Looking in the rearview mirror at Kiko, the marine asked, "You guys must be tired, huh? It's a long flight from paradise!"

"Yeah," Kiko sighed. "I guess."

"You can sleep if you want. We got some time to go."

"I'm good, thanks. Don't really feel comfortable sleeping around strangers."

"Oh, right. Sure. Smart choice. Your father taught you well."

"My mom. You've probably known our dad longer than we have," Kiko retorted.

"Oh. I'm sorry..."

"So, how much longer do we have?"

"About another hour with traffic. Want me to turn up the music?"

"No thanks—I'd rather listen to her stupid Disney songs than this crap. No offense."

"None took. Maybe you'd like some of their native music here—I heard it's real relaxing to some folks. It kind of sounds like Oriental yodeling to me, but it's okay here and there," he bargained, changing the channel to a song she was familiar with, Miruku Munari, a popular song she heard every year at Okinawan festivals.

"Oriental yodeling, huh?" Kiko scoffed.

It was as if she couldn't help but nod her head side to side, like basic instinct, as if quietly singing along melted away all of her problems. She reminisced on all the festivals she went to in Hawai'i with her mom, Yuki, and Tutu. She remembered sitting in the audience waiting patiently for her mother to play koto or sanshin on stage, dancing or singing, catching her between costume changes to cheer her on for a great show. Suddenly his stupid "oriental yodeling" comment didn't bother her anymore. It didn't matter if he understood it or not. She did and to her, it was all that mattered.

Ahead of a long line of traffic, the military base gate guards inspected incoming vehicles, while alongside the cars was the heavy presence of protesters holding signs and throwing fists in the air.

"What's going on out there?" Kiko and Yuki asked at the same time, looking at each other as if impressed they shared the same thought.

"The people here are always up in arms about something or another. But last night, a girl got hurt pretty bad, and they're upset about it is my guess—just do your best to ignore it. As long as they don't start making a scene, we don't have to worry about anything," he remarked, almost resentful to their presence, watching them like a hawk.

"What happened to the girl?" Yuki inquired, confused and scared. "And why are they mad at you?"

"They're not mad at me; they're mad at our uniforms. They think because one person is an idiot and does something stupid, all of us are criminals. But then they whine about why we don't spend money in their economy. It's just ridiculous. They're just ridiculous," he huffed.

"But didn't we invade a ton of countries cuz of one bad guy too? Doesn't that mean we're ridiculous too?" Kiko argued.

The car got quiet. Deathly quiet. Jackson spoke briefly to the gate guard, and finally, after what felt like forever, they arrived at a small lane of portables and parked.

He left the car running and stood outside to smoke a cigarette, checking his phone now and then before throwing the butt to the ground and entering the building. Within moments, he exited with their dad, who appeared older and balder than the pictures. He walked with a limp, and Kiko could tell the injury was recent from the way he was still learning to shift his weight when he moved, similar to when she injured her leg diving years before.

He waved from the door of the portable office and began walking toward the car. In her excitement, Yuki jumped out of the car and ran arms first into their dad, jumping into his hug with glee.

"Daddy!" exclaimed Yuki.

"Yuki, you're so big!" He let out in laughter as he lifted her up as high as he could. "And a heavy little dumpling too!"

"That's cuz I'm going through a growth spurt! See! See!" Yuki let out, flexing her small muscles.

Kiko, ever hesitant and full of resentment, stayed in the car, peering at her father with skepticism and apathy. As Yuki began chasing a stowaway cat hiding under the portable, their father lit a cigarette, glancing from time to time at the car as if to give Kiko some time to come out on her own terms.

Gross, Kiko thought. Mom would be pissed if she saw him smoking around Yuki. Why are we even here? She plugged her headphones back in, pulled over her hoodie, and leaned against the car window. She didn't care if it was hot enough to boil off her skin; her skin was already boiling from being here.

"You gonna come out and say hi to your old man?" he asked, knocking on Kiko's window. She looked at him with a raised eyebrow, holding up her phone as if she had better things to do.

"Tired huh? Hungry?" he asked, hoping to get anything verbal out of her. "Yup, just like your mama!" he chuckled. "Private, take these kids to a Mickey D's and get them something to munch on. I'll wrap up over here," he said, throwing his cigarette off to the side before heading back in.

Jackson sneered. "Yeah, cool. Maybe I can starch and press your boxers too?"

Kiko couldn't help but overhear him and smile—maybe he isn't such an insensitive jerk after all.

What was supposed to be a few minutes of "wrapping up" turned into another hour of waiting. Private Jackson decided his best form of revenge was to amp the kids up with sugar and goodies. The girls were thankful for the ice cream cones and McFlurries on a hot day and the mouthwatering chicken nuggets Kiko longed for after the disappointing meal on the flight.

"Ahh," sighed Yuki lovingly, staring cross-eyed into her burger. "Heaven!"

"How are you still hungry? You just ate." Kiko asked, a little upset with herself for not ordering more food on her dad's tab. "Some of us haven't eaten all day!"

Jackson laughed at Kiko's small fury and handed her his leftover nuggets. "Take mine. I could lay off this stuff for a while. The wife says it's poison anyway."

"Oh. Thanks," Kiko said, giving him side-eye. "What is it you do around here anyway?"

"Aside from babysitting? Mostly computer work. I make things go boom." He smirked, expanding his hands out like a bomb.

Finally, their father could be seen leaving the office, telling everyone he'd see them at "0600 hours on Monday" before escorting the girls to his Jeep Wrangler-like mini SUV and taking off into the incoming darkness. "You girls ready? It's gonna be a long drive home!"

Sweet Baby Buddha, Kiko thought. Seriously? Exhausted from all of the travel and worn out from all of the questions she had held inside, all the anger she had harbored, Kiko decided to take a page out of Yuki's handbook and get some sleep. Anything that meant not having to talk to Major General Shackles.

Are We There Yet?

Their father drove into the night, listening to the radio playing Okinawan eisaa. He hummed along, singing the words as best as he could. His fingers, like bachi sticks at the wheel, beat to the same rhythm of the teeku drums, an instrument unique to the islands. He even mimicked some of the dance moves he remembered from the beginning of his deployment.

The music was the first thing that drew his younger, more impressionable self into the culture and heritage of the people around him. Growing up in the American South, he knew all about parades and shows, but as he was stationed further and further from home, his eyes opened to a world he had been denied all his life. In the heat of the disco era, the people of Okinawa were dispassionate to the onslaught of the American military occupying their islands and the violence against its people since World War II.

However, once a year, without a doubt, the Shimanchu, or local Okinawans, would gather and crowd the streets. Performers dressed to the tens in traditional and contemporary kimonos, yukatas, and hapis. But eisaa was the music that got the people moving—the drums beat through the streets as if it were the heartbeat of the Loochoo Kingdom. This was the time to celebrate their people. This was their call to bring their ancestors back. It could be felt all through the streets.

He and his buddies would attend the parade and cheer on the dancers, performers, and join in during the bon dance, where the young and old gathered, encircling a large, red Yagura Gumi tower lit up with paper lanterns. As dance clubs instructed the hand gestures to each song, locals and foreigners alike joined the party train and shouted out heeshi in a call and response game of lyrics. It was only after he met their mom that he learned what this festival meant, who it was really for. He even started taking up taiko classes to impress her.

Every year, like clockwork, he would remember.

"Ha'i'ya'i'ya'sa'sa… hop… hop… hop!" he sang aloud passionately, before remembering his daughters were in the back seat, sleeping. Before he remembered she was really gone. He quickly glanced to the back seat, slightly embarrassed, adjusting his rearview mirror to see the girls, who were now waking up.

Kiko could only manage to open one eye and used it to peer at her father with anger and exhaustion, but she was a bit amused at the idea of their dad singing a song she grew up dancing to.

"Hey! You're awake—good stuff, we should be there soon!" He smiled, looking hopeful.

"At grandma's?" Kiko asked impatiently.

"Well, no. But we'll be at the docks soon. How do you like boats? They normally don't leave this late, so I had to call in a favor. Not long, about a thirty-minute boat ride to Taketomi from here. Hopefully, she's still awake," he rattled on. "Hey, check out that moon! Pretty cool huh?"

Yuki yawned. "We get to go on a boat?" She rubbed her eyes awake. "Are there sharks where we're going? Kiko are you going to be okay?"

"As long as you don't goof around, you won't have to worry about sharks. Right, Kiko?"

"I don't even care. I just want to take a shower and go to sleep." Kiko groaned, riddled with exhaustion from over twenty hours of travel.

Fortunately, they were fully awake by the time they arrived at the docks and boarded the small boat crewed by a father and son. The ride itself was pleasant, and the fresh sea air let them feel a little closer to home. Although Kiko couldn't bring herself to get close to the edge, she stayed on deck and gazed into the bright sky, missing home.

Yuki was eager to point out the faint silhouette materializing in the distance, and Kiko couldn't wait to be back on land, safe from what felt to her was a tumultuous sea. It was the first time she had been in the sea since her mother had died, and with each dip of the bow into the water, with the splash of every wave, she grew heavier and heavier, feeling sick to her stomach.

The Village is Watching

Their favorite method of travel on this day, from planes, cars, to boats, was surely the water buffalo cart ride they took to Tomi's house. The animal was an aged beauty with proud cursive-tailed horns and a deep onyx hide. The driver was an older Okinawan man in relaxed linens, who waved them on-board, welcoming them to the islands.

He sang folk tunes with a proud but strained voice as the buffalo cart moved at a steady pace through the neighborhoods. Kiko couldn't help but feel like they were being watched from the moment they set foot on the island, so using the full moon's light, she carefully examined their surroundings at every turn. She looked to the side for a brief moment and saw something move in the trees: a small figure with what appeared to be locks of hair curling down and around its arms, but just as she thought it might be grinning at her, it vanished into the branches above.

Reasoning it was nothing more than hallucinations due to sleep deprivation and jet lag, she tried to ignore these feelings of paranoia. But she couldn't help but to keep examining the forests closely as they passed, hoping to catch another glimpse. "Did anybody see that?" she asked, obviously too late.

"An, yasa!" The driver declared. "Maa yatin yuurii wundoo." Then he mimicked ghost-like movements. "Woooo," he growled in a ghoulish fashion.

Kiko tugged at Yuki's arms, thinking another set of eyes would help. Yuki though, still woozy from the boat ride, was not impressed and she looked sick to her stomach.

Yuki yanked her arm back and shouted, "Stop it!" so loud her words pierced the air like a high-pitched whistle, startling everyone on the cart, especially the driver.

"Both of you girls, cut it out!" shushed their father with an authoritative tone, like most men do when driven to the brink of their final nerve—and they were yanking a tight, thin thread.

Kiko could even see the driver raising his eyebrows as he tilted his head, maybe remembering a time his father yelled at him the same way. She swore she saw him curling a smile at the corners of his lips.

Without warning, the ox began to jerk back, forcing their bodies to sway toward the end of the cart. The driver stopped to calm him down, letting their dad know where Tomi lived, his hand gesturing to make the next right and go straight. Their dad gestured to the girls to get out and grab their things as he made his way toward the back. Helping them with their suitcases, he was sure to remind them they'd carry their luggage there.

"It's late, and if you cared enough to pack it, you'll have no problem carrying it," he insisted. "The sand is too loose to roll it—sorry."

Kiko and Yuki let out deep, annoyed sighs. "Ugh. How come he can't just bring us there?" groaned Yuki, her nose high into the sky, parallel to the ground.

"This is such bulls–" Kiko started.

"Shut your mouth! I don't know how your mom raised you, but I won't tolerate this kind of foul language," their father barked, now in full Major General Shackles mode. "Yuki—the ox was spooked, and I'm sure your whining didn't help. Now, it's just around the corner here— let's move."

"We're not soldiers," Yuki murmured, quietly enough for only Kiko to hear, to which she nodded her head in agreement and rolled her eyes so deep it made Yuki laugh.

"What's so damn funny?" Their father asked.

Kiko rolled her eyes again. "Really? I thought you don't use foul language."

He stopped, twisting his neck side to side, loud cracks echoing from his militant bones.

"I think we're here," Yuki said, easing the tension of the moment.

"What makes you say that?" Kiko asked.

"I dunno. Just a feeling."

Their father rustled through his pockets, grabbing a flashlight and a folded sheet of paper. He briefly looked down at what appeared to be an address, then up at the stone wall. He did this several times, then looked around. We're lost, Kiko thought. She noticed his eyes as the flashlight shone upon them: a piercing color, and it was only upon closer inspection that she saw they were different: a deep, forest green with hints of orange in one, and the other a cold, Icelandic blue with milky outer layers and algae-colored tints. She couldn't help but recognize them, because they stared back at her in the mirror each day.

"I think you're right, Yuki. One sec," he whispered, looking over the wall and into the property before inviting himself in.

They stood stone-stiff at an old, traditional Okinawan passing made up of thick coral hugging the property line and stopping six feet apart at the entryway. A similar wall stood proudly a few feet away, and from a distance, it appeared as though the wall wrapped around the entire estate. It made sense that it felt like a fortress because Kiko couldn't help but feel like they were being watched.

A couple of candle lanterns flickered behind the two shiisaa dogs, a couple of clay lion-dogs, one with its mouth wide open, and the other one closed. Kiko remembered what these meant, as they had similar ones outside their house in Hawai'i. Kiko was proud to recall that the left is the male, his mouth is open to ward off evil spirits. The right is the female, her mouth closed to keep good spirits inside. This seemed quite real at the moment, with Kiko feeling the heebie-jeebies and a stirring impatience as they waited for their father's return.

The moon, tinted with orange, sat above the home, showing off its almost bare-boned architecture, with only a couple of sooji screens open—as if inviting someone, anyone inside.

"You think she always leaves the doors open or just now?" Yuki asked.

Only then did Kiko see that Yuki no longer stood beside her. She was at the other side of the wall, stretching her neck chicken-like, inspecting the house.

"Yuki get back here!" warned Kiko.

Suddenly a rustling sound came from beside them. Their father, clearly frustrated, let out a calm, cool breath.

"Is anyone here?" Kiko asked.

"She may be asleep," he answered.

"Well, now what?" snarled Yuki, her body going boneless.

"One minute, one minute." Their father pointed his flashlight around hoping to gain answers or catch a passerby. Kiko couldn't help but notice a large lion-like shadow in the distance. Is that a cloud? Am I trippin? she wondered.

She peered at the figure, squinting her eyes to see into the dark, but the shadowy figure moved quickly out of view. If it were a cloud, that would be strange because there was no wind. She looked frantically around, trying to find Yuki's hand. Then she noticed one of the shiisaa had gone missing. The open-mouthed one.

"Where did the shiisaa go?" Kiko pointed toward where the figure had been moments before.

"What are you talking about?" Yuki asked, pointing at the curly-looking lion-dog statue.

Then, as if by magic, a short, hunched-over woman, wearing a white hapi and trousers appeared before them and whispered, "Mensooree."

Chills ran up Kiko's spine as she met the old woman's gaze. Her face was lit by a small paper lantern, illuminating salt and pepper hair bound tightly in a bun, and her eyes were milky, as if she were blind or had cataracts. Her hands, Kiko noticed, were tattooed with gray and greenish ink, with thick blocks, circles, and arrows.

"Holy shit, Tomi! You can't scare us like that!" blurted their father, clearly frightened.

She let out a hearty laugh and waddled back toward the house, waiting for no one, but waving "follow me" with her left hand. The arrow-like tattoos seemed to indicate the way like a compass in the night. Kiko heard Yuki's teeth chattering and took her hand. "It's okay Yuki, I'll protect you," she said.

Then together they took slow, careful steps, until finally arriving onto the wrap-around lanai, where a familiar aroma made their mouths water: Spam.

Letting the Dust Settle

Once inside the gate, they took off their shoes and placed them neatly against the side wall, except Yuki, who kicked hers off and ran toward the wafting aroma that so reminded her of home.

The melodic scent of Spam omusubi streamed into Kiko's nostrils as well, and she was so focused on her growling stomach that she hardly noticed how barren the home was until she sat down at the chabudai, a short-legged table with a small heater underneath, and took a long look around.

It was unclear if Tomi was very poor or very rich; her house was so empty, or "zen," as their mom would call it. On the floor were various tatami mats with bright green borders, and each wall appeared older than the next, haunting almost, with scrolls hanging every so often and photos of people hanging just below the ceiling. In the corner of the living room were stacks of futon mats, gently folded sheets, and beaded bamboo pillows atop them. Kiko could just barely see a small room off to the side, with its door cracked open only wide enough to see a shrine glistening inside. She looked back and forth, confused. "Is this... all of it? Where's the TV?"

Yuki shrugged and continued scarfing down the omusubi and drinking cups of frothy, cold Calpis juice, letting out a loud "Ahhh" as she finished. By the time Kiko looked down, she saw that Yuki had eaten nearly all the omusubi aside from their father, who had several as well, leaving only one for Kiko to enjoy.

She was so hungry, she ate it slowly and chewed carefully, being sure to enjoy each bite. Their father insisted the girls "hit the hay" since it was so late, and Kiko couldn't wait to finally sleep in a normal bed.

But to her dismay, when Tomi showed them their rooms, she was shocked to see the same mats they saw outside: no beds, just a tri-fold futon, and a handful of blankets. The rooms were otherwise plain, with well-worn and aging walls that made Kiko uneasy. Yuki, on the other hand, was so excited to have her own bedroom, she quickly locked the door behind her and could be heard singing playfully.

Kiko crept out of her room and lightly tapped on Yuki's door. "Psst! Yuki!"

"What!"

"Come sleep in my room. It's bigger. Just until we unpack. I don't want you sleeping by yourself tonight."

A howling wind blew over the house, shaking the sooji screen doors, and Yuki quickly fled her room with her arms full of stuffed animals, joining Kiko.

Kiko couldn't help but feel like someone was still watching them. In fact, she swore she heard a low growl in the distance, but Kiko imagined it was probably a cat or something.

"Did you hear that?" Kiko asked.

"Hear what?"

"Nothing. Never mind. It's probably just Kachan and Dad talking."

Yuki yawned. "I think you need sleep—you sound delirious. Or maybe you heard your stomach."

"Yeah," Kiko said, slightly annoyed. "I wasn't as hungry as you though. I'll just wait for breakfast. You think she knows how to make like... kid food?"

"Duh!" Yuki exclaimed quietly. "She was a mom too! Remember? She'll probably make us pancakes and sausage and... Ooo! Ooo! Maybe one of those donuts we get at the Okinawan Festival!"

"Right? Mom had to learn how to cook from someone! Hey, did you see her eyes? You think she's blind? I didn't want to ask. But I looked around and didn't see one of those stick things," Kiko said quietly.

Yuki let out a loud yawn and stretched out over the mat, tucking herself in. "I dunno, but I like her! Anyway, I'm too tired to think for another second."

"I swear, I don't know another person who eats or sleeps as much as you do, Yuki. Like how is that even possible?"

"Because I'm growing! Remember? You should sleep too unless you wanna be short forever!" Yuki said, sticking out her tongue playfully.

Kiko huffed. "Whatever. Go sleep already."

Yuki yawned again. "I love you, sissy."

"Yeah, you too," Kiko said.

"Say it!" demanded Yuki.

"I love you, too. Good night."

As if by a miracle, Yuki was soon snoring and slobbering all over her pillow. Kiko couldn't sleep, so she quietly slid open the sooji screen door to take a peek outside, squinting, hoping to catch the figure she saw earlier in the trees. The lantern inside begins to flicker, its paper cover turning into a dull orange, matching the blood moon.

Maybe you are delirious, Kiko thought, then said aloud, "I swear I saw something. I know it."

A gust of wind rushed through the trees and blew the lantern out. The room was pitch black, and Kiko couldn't see anything for a few moments until she was able to adjust to the moonlight. But she didn't feel alone, and it wasn't because of Yuki, either. Someone was out there watching her. She could feel it on her skin.

She peered for a few more moments into the vast array of moonlit silhouettes in the distance before closing the screen doors and laying down beside Yuki.

"This place is so freakin' creepy," she said to herself, staring at the ceiling. "I miss Hawai'i."

Misery Without Company

Finally, as the sun began to peek its rays over the wall, Kiko felt her eyes close tightly, snug in the comfort of the futon and full, soft comforter. It always seemed that just when she got comfortable, it was time to wake up. This is probably why she was always so grouchy, especially lately, now that sleep often meant nightmares too.

The sun, full and encroaching, now turned the cool room hot. Beads of sweat rolled down Kiko's temples as she slept, tossing, mumbling, and breathing heavily all at once. What was tamed hair the previous night was now thick and curly, with "Ryukyu baby hairs" encircled on her nape, beneath her ears, and on her forehead. Ill-tempered and sleep-deprived, Kiko moaned and groaned with frustration, before using the pillow to muffle her discontent.

Slowly sitting up, she stared blankly around the room. She saw that Yuki was gone and her bed left messy, as always. She took time to neatly fold the sheets and futons before placing them into the corner they had retrieved them from the night before. Then with a loud yawn and cat-like stretches, she padded into the kitchen. Yuki was already eating from what appeared to be a random feast at the small table, while seated on thin, taupe cushions.

Looking down, holding her hungry stomach, Kiko couldn't help but feel disappointed at the layout. A traditional Okinawan breakfast: bowls of rice, somen, miso soup, thick cuts of bright yellow takuan, leftover gooyaa champuruu, and hard scrambled eggs with anchovies littered throughout like furikake. Beside it was a cup of hot tea and a cold, perspiring glass of hibiscus juice, a popular Taketomi beverage.

"Ee, Kiko-chan. Naa ukitii?" Tomi said smiling, wishing her a good morning.

"Hey, sleepyhead! Check it out! It's not pancakes, but it sure is good!" Yuki spoke eagerly, pleasantly full from the dishes set out before her.

It always seemed like Yuki could eat anything, so in comparison, it always made Kiko seem picky. But there was little falsehood to be made, as Yuki would eat anything, say anything, or do anything to be everyone's favorite. To avoid being hated right away by their estranged grandmother, Kiko hesitantly and reluctantly began to eat. Meanwhile, Yuki was going for seconds or thirds, shoving the food into her mouth.

"Gachimayaa!" Tomi snorted, laughing feverishly.

The girls looked at her, confused, and Kiko wished she knew what she was saying or at the very least could use her phone to translate, that was if she could at all. She knew Uchinaaguchi was an old language, but having not known Japanese, Kiko didn't know if they had a lot in common.

Tomi looked un-phased by the language barrier, quietly sipping her tea with eyes closed but smiling mischievously. Then without much notice, she stood up, walked over to the room with the shrine, and closed the sooji screen.

Soon, Tomi was praying in what sounded like a hurried, almost mumbling pace. Kiko inched closer, trying to hear if she might recognize it.

Their mother practiced Buddhism too, but this was unlike any chanting of gongyo she knew. Kiko listened closely for the famous daimoku, "Nam Myoho Renge Kyo," she had memorized over the years at youth division meetings at their local Sokka Gakkai International Center, but it was difficult to make out what Tomi was saying. It sounded almost conversational, as though she was talking to herself. Kiko couldn't recognize the cadence or the words. Maybe she was a different kind of Buddhist?

Kiko cracked the sooji screen open to find her grandmother's fierce and seemingly blind gaze upon her. She jolted back, falling like a scrambling crab before managing to get back to her feet. She didn't like how ominous and eerie their grandmother was. It was like being characters in a horror film. Except it was in their lives, not a movie, and they were thousands of miles away from the only person who knew of their whereabouts.

Speaking of movies and whereabouts, there were no movies, and neither Kiko nor Yuki were able to place their location on a map. So their imaginations spit fire at a feverish pace. Kiko kept thinking up all the ways they were going to die, whether being poisoned by Tomi because she couldn't see and mixed bleach or rat poison into their food instead of seasonings, or just based on the food—starvation. Kiko could swear something fishy was going on, and she was going to get to the bottom of it.

Yuki, on the other hand, was familiarizing herself with the house, opening and shutting doors, cabinets, and drawers wherever she went. Somehow, the house being so open and empty made it seem larger and labyrinth-like. The large screen doors could transform the house from a studio to a four-bedroom, or inside to outside. Kiko was noticing how it made the house feel easy to get lost in. Then all of a sudden, she asked herself, where is their father?

She figured he slept in, but he was nowhere to be found. Did he leave? When? Why didn't he say goodbye? Infuriated, she went back into the room to grab her phone and then began to hunt the premises for reception. Seriously? No signal? What kind of place has no signal? We're going to die. This is how it ends. Of course. Why else would you be in the middle of nowhere? Oh my god!

Her hands stretched further and further, and her feet stacked up on her tippy toes, until she finally gave up. She found some comfort in knowing a few games still functioned before learning Tutu never packed her charger. Searching for one in Yuki's luggage, Kiko felt defeated and was left empty-handed. She couldn't even call their father to yell at him. In fact, she couldn't recall that he had left his number with them either. It was as if he couldn't wait to get rid of them, and Kiko wondered why Tomi and Yuki didn't say anything about his disappearance. It was difficult to pinpoint what about this situation wasn't suspicious. Because everything at this point felt weird, this whole place seemed unreal.

Trying to remember what day it was, she wondered if there was a library nearby. She needed to find a way for them to communicate aside from grunts and gestures or attempting to play charades with a blind old woman. I mean, who knows if she isn't deaf, too? Kiko felt guilty for even thinking that. But she just couldn't understand why their father would just drop them off with someone who needed to be cared for, and not someone who could care for them. In fact, she was eager to wake up earlier the next day to see exactly how she managed to cook.

It wasn't long before Kiko grew bored of her cyclical thoughts and went out to check on Yuki and Tomi, who were in the garden tending to the plants.

"Hey! Did you see Dad leave?" Kiko shouted as she walked outside to join them.

"Nope! He left before I woke up! Why?" Yuki yelled back.

"Oh," Kiko said, disappointed to be the last one to know.

Kiko waved her hands above her face to catch Yuki's attention, then cupped her mouth and whispered so quietly Yuki had to squint to read Kiko's lips asking if she "speaks English."

"She can't see, Kiko, but she can hear us," Yuki spoke plainly, using the same gesture mockingly.

Kiko's eyes widened with outrage and embarrassment. "Can she understand us?" she whispered carefully, just in case.

"Nope," replied Yuki. "Well, actually, I dunno. I can understand her just fine somehow. Can't you? It's like I know what she's saying, but I don't. It's mostly just pointing at things and figuring it out, you know?"

Kiko didn't know. She always struggled with languages, even body language. She had difficulty passing English, math, and music on account of her dyslexia. She summed it up to her hating all of those courses and learned enough tips and tricks to pass with C's this year, with A's in Agriculture and Woodshop.

In fact, she was "Gardner of the Year" and got second prize in Shop class for the butsudan, a shrine inscribed with "Nam Myoho Renge Kyo," she made for her mom. She only lost on account that they weren't allowed to do religious crafts, but she was happy to be docked the points, in her efforts to make the gift.

Realizing she had zoned-out into a random stream of thought, she shook her head vigorously like a wet dog and focused on their activity: pruning leaves. It was meditative. Their mom used to use it for punishment, but Kiko had always enjoyed it. Besides, it helped to keep her mind off of everything going on. She admired Tomi's vast array of herbs, flowers, and trees and wondered how a blind woman could take care of it all. Kiko took the liberty of transplanting a couple of the flowers to more suitable companions before she grew bored and returned inside to give her phone another try.

No matter how many times she turned her phone on and off, trolled through her settings, and desperately searched the house for any kind of wire or router that could connect her back to the real world, it was to no avail. She was stuck. And with her sister, who she'd now be forced to entertain. "I hate my life," Kiko said coarsely under her breath as she sat at the chabudai and stared blankly at the now cold food. She felt utterly defeated.

The day was hot, and Kiko wasn't planning on staying inside any longer. She yelled out her sister's name and whistled, as one would to get a dog's attention, until Yuki trotted into the doorway of the main space. Yuki appeared excited that Kiko wanted to hang out with her but also looked like she was doing her best to contain herself because she knew over-excitement normally made Kiko irritated to the point of no longer wanting to play. But there just had to be something to do around here besides chores.

"Let's go holoholo," Kiko said casually, tying her shoes.

"Did you ask grandma?"

"Brah. Seriously? She can't even see us! Plus, this island has like twenty houses. I think we'll be okay." Kiko said it with so much sarcasm and confidence that it would be impossible for Yuki to not comply.

"I keep forgetting that!" squeaked Yuki, pursing her lips to hold in her laughter. "Okay, let me get my camera."

The island of Taketomi was, in fact, quite small. Kiko remembered Googling it on the drive over and learning that there were only about three-hundred people that lived there, and that it only takes an hour or so to walk around the island. The houses had traditional red-roofs and all different kinds of shiisaa dogs made up of broken tiles and bits of clay. Each house looked different and, in that sense, unique.

It didn't take long before the girls made it to the town center and saw a few bento shops open. Hoping they accepted yen, the Japanese currency, Yuki and Kiko nervously tapped at the bits of coinage in their pockets as they searched for something to quench their thirst. They sat on the corner and watched the water buffalos carting tourists to and from the shallow waters.

"Tourists look the same everywhere, yeah?" Kiko asked.

"Right?" Yuki said, striking a pose and pretending to take a "selfie."

"Isn't it weird that there are like... no other kids here?" complained Kiko.

"You think so?"

Unfortunately, this was something Kiko hoped to be wrong about but wasn't. As they walked through the neighborhoods, there wasn't a kid in sight that didn't belong to a visiting tourist. Getting lost in the labyrinth-like layout of the land, it took them much longer to get home than anticipated.

Dinner was fish, rice, and miso soup. Simple and cold. The girls could hear Tomi in the other room with a guest, and they wouldn't see her until right before they were getting ready to go to bed. Between the long walk and the jet lag, sleep would come easy for both of them.

However, for Kiko, the waterfall of memories poured over her dreamscape, and suddenly she was drowning all over again. She felt like she could not breathe, as if something was sitting on top of her, weighing down her chest. If her eyelids could speak, they would have several voices, each of them calling out to her, as if to lure her into the darkness of the night. Sweating and shivering, she woke up to an empty room, her door slightly ajar, as if something, or someone, was inside.

In a panic, Kiko jumped to her feet and ran outside, using her cellphone as a light. She saw something running off into the distance, and her heartbeat began to race. It was then that Kiko managed to catch her breath and realize she was alone, in the woods of a city she didn't know, chasing some lurking creature with nothing more than a cellphone that didn't even work on this island. Fear crept into every inch of her body.

Looking around with her phone, she could only manage to see one small area at a time. A pain gripped her insides, like she knew something bad was coming. A crackling of branches was enough to make her jump out of her skin, and she watched in terror as her phone flew from her hand and hit the ground. This was no place to be alone in the dark, it occurred to her, and she sure as hell didn't want to die like this.

Under a small bundle of leaves, she saw her phone's light shining and frantically reached out to grab it before a branch snapped loudly, and when Kiko looked up, she swore she saw a child-like figure, with what appeared to be dreadlocks, staring back at her in the darkness.

In a panic, she screamed and sprinted towards the direction of Tomi's house, desperately trying not to scream and failing to keep her

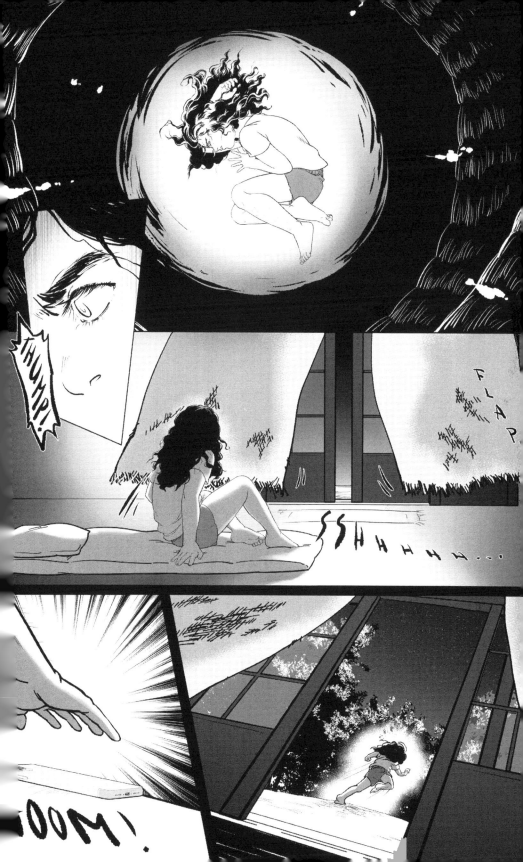

panic under control. "Nope! Nope! Not today, Satan! No! No! No!" Kiko muttered over and over.

After what felt like eons of running, Kiko finally arrived safely indoors again. Her thoughts were racing: Was that a stupid boy playing tricks on her? How did he even get inside? I should have taken a picture! Ughhh!

Hoping to calm herself down, Kiko reflexively reached into her back pocket to get her phone, only to remember: it was out there. Her heart sank. She felt as if she were going to puke at any moment. All of her pictures. All of her music and phone numbers and games. Everything, gone.

Afraid to go back outside, Kiko tried to convince herself nobody else could be up at this hour, and she would just stay up and wait for the sun to come out before setting off to find her phone. This was quite possibly the worst end to the worst day. After everything she had been through, she had lost the only solace afforded in her existence.

I

Insomnia and Insanity

As Kiko waited for the sun to chase out the morning twilight, she heard Tomi shuffle across the tatami mats. She was so alert, she could tell when even the smallest lost tethers caught Tomi's tabi socks, causing a small skip of her step. This is it, Kiko thought. I'm going to see how she cooks. Quietly rolling off the futon mat and ninja-stepping across the mats, walking heel-to-toe like the movies, she entered the foyer.

"Ukimisoochi," Tomi said ever so gently.

Assuming she said good morning, Kiko responded. "Ohiyo gozaimasu."

"Ee," Tomi waved her hand. "Uuh-kee-mee-soo-chee-tai."

"Ukimi...soo...chi—thai!" Kiko said, spitting out the last of the syllables proudly.

To her surprise, food was already made, and all that was left on the stove was soup brimming near the edge of the pot, which prompted Tomi to turn off the stove.

"Jootoo. Nintan naa?" she asked Kiko, using her hands to reference sleep. Kiko studied her body and face before piecing it all together.

"Yeah, I couldn't sleep well." Kiko proceeded to set up the table while Tomi prepared tea. She couldn't help but stare at the greenish-black ink that stained the better part of her grandmother's hands. Tomi then prepared small sardine-like fish, seaweed, carrot kinpira, toofu and eggs with shirasu (a small anchovy-like fish) after handing Kiko a bittermelon and knife. Kiko assumed she wanted her to cut it and clean it out. But before she even began, Tomi pointed toward the sink and rubbed her hands together to signal "wash it first."

After cutting off the stems and ends, like she did most vegetables she helped her mom prepare, she remembered to rub salt on the bittermelon to make it taste more bearable. She returned to the cupboards and found salt but also shelves of strange seasonings, hanging dried herbs, tinctures, and odd reptiles soaking in large sealed jars. Although it made Kiko raise an eyebrow, she returned back to the table and began to cut away.

Tomi waved her hand "stop" and showed Kiko how to cut it properly, using gentle wave-like motions.

You're blind! Kiko thought, letting out a deep, annoyed sigh.

When they sat down to eat, Tomi showed her the significance of each dish, as if differentiating them by weight or shape on the assorted plates. "Goo-yaa," she said, pointing at her heart, as if for longevity. "Toofu," she said, making a circling gesture at the fishy egg scramble then flexing her wrinkled muscles and pointing at her skin, suggesting skin and muscle vitality. Finally, she held the small carrot kinpira bowl next to her eyes to suggest they help with vision.

"Which one is this again?" Kiko pointed to the gooyaa champuruu, trying to trick Tomi into revealing she was not really blind, only to receive a devilish smile instead as she reached her hand out over the table with mild confusion, accidentally knocking a bowl over. Kiko grabbed a rag to clean up the mess and took a longer look at Tomi's hands, examining each shape that trailed along her fingers and up to her wrists.

Gently placing her finger on the back of Tomi's hand, Kiko asked, "What does this mean?"

"Hajichi," Tomi said.

"Huh?"

"*Hajichi*," she said again.

Although Kiko wanted to ask so many questions, she struggled to use the little Japanese she knew as Tomi constantly referred to its Okinawan counterpart. So instead, Kiko just finished her scrambled eggs with tazukuri, a candied sardine, rice, and tea before returning to her room to get ready. Kiko was still rather disappointed with the clothes Tutu packed, confusing her good clothes for the ones she'd begun to outgrow and planned to donate.

Sighing deeply and frequently, she put on her outdated blue Kailua Intermediate T-shirt and her old overall shorts she would wear to lo'i patches on her adventures with La'akea. It was the closest thing she had to hiking clothes, and she planned to scour the forest until she found her phone. She had hoped that she turned off the flashlight setting before dropping it but couldn't be sure, as she had trouble recollecting the exact turn of events detail-for-detail.

"Nuu soo ga?" Tomi asked, conveniently waiting outside Kiko's room, handing over a small bento box of fish heads, rice, and black ties of wet, glossy seaweed.

"Huh?" Kiko asked, thinking Tomi was asking where she was going. "I'm going out," Kiko said, miming what she was planning to do before forgetting Tomi couldn't see. She repeated herself again, more slowly, as if it would magically be translated upon hearing it this way. Tomi simply nodded, handed her the bento, and left for her prayer room, sliding the sooji screen shut behind her.

When Kiko heard her grandmother chanting, she slid out the back and attempted to retrace her steps. Trying to ignore the pungent smell of fissured fish heads within the small cloth wrappings, she pushed forward, returning to the forest. Out of nowhere, Kiko heard a crackling of leaves behind her and jerked back, dropping the food, only to find Yuki, still in her pajamas, following her.

"Yuki! Go back!" Kiko hissed.

"Why? What are you doing?" Yuki asked with curious malevolence.

"Nothing! Just go back. Now."

"No. I'm not going unless you come with me."

Frustrated, Kiko gave up. Someone must have stolen it, but who? When?

"What you looking for?" Yuki asked.

"Nothing. Let's go."

Yuki pointed behind Kiko. "Is it that?"

"Oh, shoot." Kiko looked back at the smelly bento. "I'll get it later. It's fine," she said, unable to bear the thought of walking with it again.

As they returned to the house, Kiko thought Yuki was up to her tricks again because she kept saying she felt like someone was watching them. Yuki loved to scare Kiko, who didn't take much to get chicken skin. But in the back of her mind, Kiko couldn't help but feel like Yuki only validated her paranoia because she felt as though they were being watched too. In fact, all the way up to the gate, it felt like they were being followed. Kiko nudged Yuki to go inside before taking a final look at their surroundings and heading in too.

The day dragged on into the evening. But still adjusting to the new time zone, Kiko and Yuki were in bed before the sun went down. It was a humble reminder that although it felt like so much time had already passed, they were still in the beginnings of their new life.

At night, Kiko dreamed of the water again, of her mom's hand slipping further away. She felt like she couldn't breathe and gasped for air, only to wake and see a small, almost troll-like man with the face of a child, and deep red dreadlocks that wrapped around his body like rope and armor. His irises, as yellow as sunflowers, peered into her waking eyes inquisitively as he sat on her chest, smiling.

But when he stretched the corners of his lips, and his mouth opened slightly, it was impossible not to notice his large, sharp teeth that could probably snap her neck with a single bite. His face was lit at an angle, like how someone telling a scary story around a campfire does, and it was then she noticed he had what she had been looking for: her phone.

Motionless and struggling for oxygen, Kiko attempted to use her hands to tell him she couldn't breathe. But he only mirrored her gesture, letting out a sharp cry of pain as he jumped off like a spider, stepping back with apprehension.

"That's... my... cell... phone!" Kiko gasped, trying to speak between heavy breaths while lunging toward it. Like a child holding a new toy, the creature snapped his hands back so quickly and moved so fervently that Kiko decided to just sit down and try to reason with him.

She spoke slowly, using downward hand motions to calm him. "I... will... not... hurt you. I just want that..." She pointed at the phone, bringing her hands to her chest like it held a treasure inside.

In the light, he appeared much taller, around Yuki's height, his shadow growing larger on the wall as he got to his feet and pointed the flashlight directly at her. Kiko yelped as he drew closer and closer before finally gaining such closeness, so quickly, Kiko jumped when he was but a breath away from her, reeking of fish.

"Nuu ya ga, kunu hichatooru haku gwaa?" he grunted, shining the bright light at her again and violently shaking the phone in her face.

She finally saw what the problem was: the Face ID was locked. And when she looked into the now cracked front-facing camera, it opened, showing the wallpaper of her, Yuki, and their mom at Waimea Falls. It surprised her, and she was further surprised when he ripped it away from her face and dashed into the corner where he looked at the image with concerned curiosity, his finger touching the screen as if petting one of the faces.

Kiko slowly moved toward him, tip-toeing before a creaking sound from outside spooked him off into the night. Scared and exhilarated, she stepped outside the screen door and peered into the forest. He had left as mysteriously as he had appeared.

She stayed awake in bed, staring at her ceiling until reality and fantasy pinwheeled into the same rabbit hole, and she began to feel its dizzying effects—so exhausted she could hardly move. "It was just a dream," Kiko repeated over and over, until morning when she heard Yuki shriek with excitement.

Yuki burst through the door with a handful of andaagii, mochi, and rice paper candies announcing "It's Children's' Day! Look what we got!" With joyful liberation, they stuffed their mouths with the sweet treats.

Tomi used the day to take the girls out and about, stopping by the craft center to make small shiisaa dog clay figurines, which only Yuki finished, and picking up any snack their hearts desired from the local sweets shop. All over town, people gifted items to the girls, and they felt so special that Kiko could hardly remember she had lost her phone. She didn't realize the perks that came with being the only children on the island until now, but even Tomi was getting gifts from neighboring folks and store clerks.

Kiko wondered how her grandmother must have survived being blind all these years and figured maybe they saw her as a child, regardless of age, and gave her gifts because of this disability. She was also curious why she insisted on wearing an all-white hapi and linens everywhere she went, and then changed into to her homely robe with a moth-like design on its back upon returning home. But for now, Kiko was crashing from the day's intake of sugars and was eager to go home and sleep off her restless thoughts and sore legs.

To her excitement, she walked into her room to find her cellphone placed on her folded futon. Beside it was the bento box she had left in the forest, now full of fish and kelp. Suddenly she remembered everything from the night and couldn't believe it had escaped her all day. She unlocked the phone and sighed with great relief, going straight to the photo gallery and seeing with her very own eyes, the creature's blurred selfies of shock, horror, and childlike confusion.

He looked much more like a child in the photos, but she remembered his voice sounded deep and scruffy, like an older man. Tattoos stretched across his face and body and the dreadlocked, fibrous red hairs wrapped around his shoulders like a rappel rope. Eager to show Tomi and Yuki, Kiko darted into the kitchen with the bento box and threw out her arm, phone in hand, only to stare at blank faces.

"Your screen is black," Yuki giggled.

"Oh!" Kiko turned it around, but the screen was indeed black—as in dead.

"What were you trying to show us? Well..." Yuki said, nodding toward Tomi, "Me?"

"Nothing," Kiko said, disappointed. "Never mind."

Yuki laughed. "You look crazy. I think you need to go shi-shi nai-nai already."

"You're telling me. Good night."

Tomi cleared her throat, pointing at the bento box. Kiko had no idea how she knew she had it but felt uneasy in returning it to her now. She wondered if maybe, just maybe, she knew what was going on all along. With great reluctance, she handed it over, glaring into Tomi's eyes as if making sure she was blind for real, for real. But Tomi just smiled, placing the box's new contents into a small jar on the counter and the empty box in the sink.

"But wait. Did you know? How?" Kiko hardly managed to process her racing thoughts.

"Go. To. Sleep!" Yuki roared. She looked at Tomi for a sign of approval.

But Kiko couldn't sleep. She tried, even pretended just to see him return, but he never did. Her mind was racked with questions, too many questions, and even she knew she needed to get some rest before she went insane.

Alienation Creates Allies

The days would begin to pass quickly, and without all the distractions, it was rather easy for the girls to slip into their new routine. In fact, Kiko was even starting to get used to the food with the help of their weekly visits to the store to get a snack or two. Tourism started to get busier as both Japanese and European schools were letting out around this time. Bustles of travelers would make their half-day stay and lazily lounge on the carts as the drivers sang old folk songs while strumming their sanshin, a three-stringed Okinawan lute made with black lacquered wood, snake-skin, and which required horned-tipped finger picks to play.

Just to keep it interesting, they made it a point to go into town every day after they helped Tomi around the house. For a place that felt rather empty, there were a lot of random things that needed upkeep, especially after visitors. The girls often thought Tomi found it to be a game. She would just point at things blindly and summon them to do whatever it was she needed, whether it was tending the garden, raking the sand and rocks, or helping in the kitchen, with a simple wave of her hand.

Meanwhile, Tomi would be meeting with guests in the small room she prayed in, which could vary anywhere from a few hours to all day.

After they gallivanted about the town, they would often return home to some hibiscus tea and bentos made by Tomi, who was always found in the kitchen concocting one thing or another, while proudly singing local tunes. Normally, the girls would get to meet Tomi's nearly daily guests to enjoy a meal together, as Yuki, making long strides learning Uchinaaguchi, attempted to engage in light conversation using her new language skills. As a matter of fact, despite mispronouncing some words now and then, she would often boast it around, greeting tourists and locals alike.

Kiko, on the other hand, used her free time in the internet cafe to look up more information about the island, its folklore, and especially its yuurii or spirits (both good and evil), hoping to gain some sort of advantage or insight into the energy she felt all around her and the red-headed man-boy that left her sleeplessly aggravated and distraught. Upon meticulously placing and replacing words in the search box, she finally came about a yokai site that detailed all of the Loochoo folklore, demons, and spirits who walked the earth.

"That's the kijimunaa. They're rare to meet, but I heard we have a few on this island," proclaimed a voice behind Kiko.

She turned quickly, angered by whoever was hovering about, only to see a short, skinny Okinawan boy with a bowl haircut, black high socks, and even higher shorts standing proudly with a handful of books.

"Hey! You're from America, huh? I can tell!"

Kiko frowned. "What makes you say that?"

"Well, for one. You are using the English setting. But you look shima-haafu, so I figured military kid. We have the most American military bases outside of the Americas, so you must be American."

Wow, way to play Sherlock Holmes, kid, Kiko thought, shooting him a thumbs up. "What's shima-haafu?"

"Oh, it means half-half. I couldn't tell if you were Okinawan or Japanese at first," he blurted before staring at Kiko's hairy arms. "But now that I'm looking at you—definitely Shimanchu." He laughed loudly and briefly, before realizing he was the only one to do so. "I am Kyoshi. I live here on-island. Well, sometimes. Mostly for breaks. My parents teach at the college, so I stay here with my grandparents."

"Well, your English is pretty good for being raised here," Kiko said. "Do your parents teach you, or did you learn in school?"

"My mom teaches at the American schools, so I learned from her. She said the more languages the better. I speak Japanese, Mandarin, English, and Uchinaaguchi. Uchinaaguchi is from my grandparents. They always say, 'Nmarijima nu kutuba wasshiinee kunin washiin,'" Kyoshi said, waving his finger around in imitation of his grandparents. "To forget your native tongue means to forget your native country."

"That's actually pretty cool. My sister, Yuki, is learning Uchinaaguchi. I suck at it, so just English for me."

"That's too bad. 'You limit yourself by only speaking one' as my mother always says."

Kiko felt the urge to slap him. "So, do you only speak in other people's words? You don't think that's limiting yourself too?"

"Um, I guess," he said, dropping his head. "Well, goodbye."

"Wait—what else do you know about these..." She pointed at the computer screen. "Uh, kijimura?"

"Kiji-moo-nah," he corrected.

"Right. That."

"Are you sure you don't mind me quoting people?"

Kiko rubbed her neck. "Wow, I'm sorry, okay? Can you just please answer my question?"

"Well, what do you want to know?"

"Ugh! Never mind. Jeez Louise, brah." Kiko huffed and turned back to the computer.

"Well," Kyoshi said after a few seconds.

"You're still here? I said never mind!"

"Do you want to know or not?" he hissed. "Kijimunaa are rare yuurii. They only interact with a few people. They look about our age and have thick, red hair and mud-red skin but are super old. You can tell by their —" He stopped, pointing at his private parts.

"Eww!" Kiko groaned.

"Well anyway, they are tricksters, see—they like to help, but for a price. And once you become their friend, you can *never* go back on your word. They are terribly jealous; I heard they've slaughtered whole farms and burned down villages because they felt ignored."

"How do you know so much?"

"Because my ufuufutanmee—that's great-great-grandfather—was cursed by one. See, my ufuufutanmee befriended a kijimunaa, and he helped him become a fisherman. Anyway, eventually, he met my great-great-grandmother, and they got married. The kijimunaa got so jealous, he started taking all the fish, and my great-great-grandparents became poor. They couldn't eat, and she died in childbirth because she was so sick from starvation. Then the kijimunaa used their baby as leverage to regain my ufuufutanmee's friendship, and, because he knew the consequences, he agreed."

"Then what happened?" Kiko asked, excited to hear more.

"And until he died, they fished together. The kijimunaa even helped to raise my ufuutanmee, my great-grandfather, who still leaves out fish eyes and fresh rice for him almost every day."

"Wait, he's still alive? He sees them?" Kiko cried out, hoping this was the answer to her problems.

"Yeah, he's alive. He doesn't speak much. My mom says he has dementia so not to bother him. But he loves talking about the kijimunaa. I'm sure if you wanted, he would tell you too. But he hasn't been feeling well lately." He stared into the middle distance, lost in thought.

"Kyoshi-chan!" a nearby voice called out. "Yuntakuu! Rikka."

"Sorry, I got to go!" Kyoshi said and quickly ran away.

"Bye!" Kiko yelled, as he disappeared from her vision.

Going back to the computer seemed difficult, now that she heard from a real local about it. But she prevailed in her studies to find out even more, such as the fact that kijimunaa can appear to live just like the locals, even having kids; nevertheless, they loved snapper fish heads and fish eyes, preferably the left one, and hated octopus. Farting makes them go away, Kiko noted, smirking devilishly to conceal her internalized laughter. At last, she finally found the most pertinent information.

"They like to sit on... the chests of people sleeping..." she read out loud, "or blow out candle light in the... evening hours." The sudden pain in her chest returned. That's right, she thought. He was sitting on my chest! He was using my phone. Maybe he thought it was a candle and he wanted to blow it out! Kiko couldn't help but draw several kinds of conclusions to her nightmarish dilemma, but she also felt excited. Like all the anime and magic books she had read at Yuki's age were real. Maybe it wasn't weird feelings she had, but magic all along. Maybe she wasn't crazy. Maybe she was just magical.

"You're a wizard, Kiko," Kiko spoke aloud, mimicking Hagrid's accent and the famous line from Harry Potter, her go-to movie when she was down. Kiko felt nothing but elated, as she printed off the papers and marched home with a smile.

Strange Happenings
(Kiko)

The walk home seemed longer than normal. It may have been that I got so caught up in reading the articles I found online that I was taking random turns instead of looking up, focusing as hard as I could before the letters danced around again. Before I knew it, I ended up at the foot of the forest the website warned me about earlier. Facing the evergreen gajumaru trees masking the thick, braided banyans that reached far toward what I could only imagine was the ocean, I swore it looked like a huge moat or wall surrounding the island.

Maybe this was where they hid. I mean, they like banyan trees, right? And I had seen him take off into the night in this direction. My nerves must have gotten the best of me because the papers became damp and wrinkled in my hands. I could feel my heart quicken, and decided to quickly head back to the village.

But I couldn't help this nagging feeling of someone watching me the whole way. I kept looking back, hoping to catch a glimpse. But nothing. No one.

Going home was a bit difficult because so many of the houses looked the same in the early evening, but I found a system. I followed the path until I saw the large, sole shiisaa dog made up of broken tiles with sharp, pointed eyes. It was sort of my own personal lighthouse, telling me our house was right around the corner.

I could smell something delicious coming from inside. Quickly untying my shoes and heading inside, I saw Yuki and Tomi putting plates of food on the table. A sudden ache in my stomach would remind me of what I had forgotten.

"Did you grab the noodles?" Yuki asked.

I had hoped nobody would mention it. "I'm sorry. I forgot," I said, looking down at my hands full of crumpled papers.

But to my surprise, they had noodles already. Tomi had made Yakisoba, my favorite dish, a savory brown fried noodle with Spam, onions, fish cake, and green onion. My mouth watered as the steam wafted throughout the room. Half-ashamed and half-starving, I helped to finish setting the chabudai and boiled some water for tea, hoping to make up for my late arrival.

Tomi pointed at the papers in a "let me see it" fashion, so I handed them over to her. She stared at the papers, and I was convinced she could see, until she brought them to her mouth and bit at the edges like a crazy person, as if to tell me, "Are these the noodles you bought? Lots of fiber I see." As she hardly spoke, it was fun to imagine her voice being anything I wanted it to be, so I just imagined it sounded like Yoda. But right now, she spoke the language of shame, and I spoke that language fluently.

"No, it's not noodles—it's research! I said I forgot. I'm sorry."

But Tomi laughed it off and gave me the papers back, hand-pressed and flattened. As we ate quietly, I could hear my stomach growling for more.

"Did you just fart?" Yuki chortled.

"No!" I scoffed, swallowing my bite. "It's just my stomach."

"Mm-hmm! Sure, it was. It's okay to fart you know. Everyone does it," Yuki snickered.

"Of course, I know that, but I didn't! It was just my stomach!"

Tomi's face became stern and cold as she looked up, pursing her lips together and a loud *brrrppphhh* exploded from under her. But nothing shook the house more than our combined laughter at her gnarly gasses, which sounded off in various tones and frequencies for minutes to follow.

"Speaking of 'flatulence' actually," I said, proud to show off the new term I learned from my research. "Did you know you can ward off kijimunaa just by farting?"

Tomi raised an eyebrow, an eerie kind of calm overwhelming her earlier cheerful disposition.

"Hmm," she said. Just *hmm*. It was a small expression that would riddle me for the rest of the night, as I told Yuki about the random pieces of folklore I picked up, and about Kyoshi, the boy I met earlier.

She was excited to hear about another kid in town. I wondered if it meant more kids would be coming and why their school got out so late into the school year. Either way, we were both looking forward to waking up early and hunting around the village to hang out with Kyoshi—Yuki, looking to make a new friend and me, looking for more answers.

Finally settling into bed, I took out the readings again and glanced over and over at the words "kijimunaa." But as my eyelids got heavier, the words got harder and harder to read, until even the paper became too heavy to carry.

I remember tossing and turning. I was back in the water, and I was struggling again, like when you try to punch in your dreams, but your arms turn to mush. It was as if I was defenseless and had no other choice but to sink into the abyss. I gasped for breath and, cracking my eyes open, a shadow leapt off my chest and ran into the corner. As I sat up and turned on the light, the small creature hurled his body over the lamp and snuffed it out. We were in the dark, alone, and the only light was the moon outside the window, framing his silhouette, leaving only his bright eyes piercing my very soul.

"Soojimu," he said.

"Soo...jimu?" I asked, doing my best to enunciate it properly despite trying to catch my breath.

"Unjoo nuu ndi iyabiiga?" he ghoulishly responded in what sounded like gibberish.

"Huh?" I asked, scared to be wrong.

Pointing at his heart, he said, "Soojimu." Then thrusting a finger at my shoulder, he asked, "Unju nu naa ya nuu ga?"

Naa means "name" in Uchinaaguchi, I remembered from Yuki's practice earlier.

"Kiko," I said, pointing at my heart.

"Ncha," he grunted, his brow snapped together disapprovingly. "Uchinaaguchi naimi?"

I couldn't understand what he was saying and just threw my hands up in defeat.

"Niibuyaa," he said, laughing. Then he drew a small bamboo vial from a pouch hidden within his grass-skirt, and took a sip before offering it to me. I refused at first, but when his face grew red hot, I grabbed the vial and swallowed its bitter contents, praying not to throw up.

"Yukuimisooree, niibuyaa," he said in a sing-songy voice before pulling the blanket over my body, patting my head light enough that his long talon-like nails snagged a few hairs before he disappeared back into the night.

And for the first time, I slept without a dream, without a nightmare. For the very first time since she died, I didn't see my mom. The guilt of that relief would haunt me for days to come.

The Awakening

Kiko woke up late into the morning, totally refreshed from her first full night of sleep. An eerie guilt nagged at her, but she couldn't ignore the satisfaction and renewed hope that came from good rest. She wondered what Soojimu put in the drink and why it had repressed any memory of dreams. She quietly and neatly folded the futon mat and feathered comforter and moved it to the corner of the room, before getting dressed and joining Yuki and Tomi in the kitchen.

To her surprise, they had eaten without her and were already prepping the next meal. The stove was full of various pots and pans, each creating a different dish. The smell was not so intoxicating, as it was a curious thing. Kiko asked Yuki how she could help, but Yuki insisted she eat because "they had a big day ahead." However, the meal consisted of little, compared to the regular feasts Tomi usually prepared, so Kiko finished anxiously, hoping it was enough to sustain her for their planned activities.

Tomi took much longer than usual getting ready. She came out dressed in a stiff, white yukata, which looked like a thinner version of a kimono. Her long, wavy, white hair was bound tightly in a kanpuu style, resting like a thick ball of yarn atop her head and held in place by a jiifaa: a long, silver hairpin, which was thick at the top and decorated with a single cherry blossom. For the first time, Kiko noticed her wearing white tabi, adorned with what appeared to be a jade necklace and a claw-like talisman, which struck her as odd.

Doesn't she worry she will get it dirty? Well, she can't see, but still? Kiko's wondered how one could even keep clothes this clean, this pure white, while even her mom struggled with daily laundering.

Nevertheless, they packed a small bag of snacks and goodies and helped Tomi lug around a cart of fruits, vegetables, herbs and what appeared to be a portable shrine made up of small stones, ancient-looking voodoo dolls, incense, a coral mortar with a stone pestle, and a small pewter cauldron-like pot.

Holy crap—we're gonna see some freakin' magic today! Kiko thought. "Where are we going?" she asked Yuki with a bit of mischief in her voice.

"We're gonna clean someone's house, I think. She mentioned something about cleansing and praying earlier."

"Huh? Cleaning? Praying? That's it? What's all this stuff for then?"

"For praying, duh! You know like what mom puts on her butsudan back home?"

"Right. Right. Okay, so where are we going?"

"I dunno. Ask Kachan!"

"Who's Kachan?"

"Oh my god, Kiko! Kachan, our grandma!"

"Well, Jesus, I didn't know! What's got you all hot and bothered?"

"Nothing. You're just being annoying today. First, you wake up late, so we had to prepare everything. Now you won't stop asking questions. Questions you could have asked if you woke up early!"

"Then why not just wake me up?"

Yuki screamed in frustration, piercing Kiko's eardrums.

"Aht! Aht! Aht!" hushed Tomi, her finger pressed against her lips.

Yuki, with bloodshot eyes and streaming tears, stormed outside to wait for them. Kiko expected the tantrum to last much longer, but Yuki was seemingly calm by the time she and Tomi joined her by the front gate.

They walked no further than a block away and entered a property that was barren, dry, and felt nothing short of cursed. Tomi signaled to wait outside the gate. Then she made her way inside to be greeted with many accolades by the home's occupants.

Stretching her neck as far as she could, Kiko could see Tomi talking to the family who were pointing at the sooji screens, the ground, the outdoor landscape, and just about everything, indicating it needed to be cleaned. Eventually, the girls were invited inside as well.

Kiko was shocked to see Kyoshi apprehensively peeping out of the hallway. She felt happy to know that at least she wouldn't be bored cleaning and could use this time to get more information about the kijimunaa and tell Kyoshi all about what happened. But Kyoshi looked sick and uneasy. In fact, he hardly even noticed Kiko's existence as he moved slowly between the kitchen and the far bedroom.

She didn't understand why he was being so distant when just the other day, he wouldn't stop bugging her. But then it hit her, as she walked down the hallway and out of the corner of her eye, she saw an old man lying on the ground. He looked deathly ill. This must be his great-grandfather, his ufuutanmee, she thought, suddenly feeling like a jerk for ever being upset over something so foolish.

"Hey, are you okay?" Kiko asked Kyoshi, who sat on the ground beside him.

"No. He's sick and we don't know what's wrong. We've tried everything, but he's getting so weak. Obaa thinks he's going to die," he added, looking longingly at his great-grandfather's face, which was wrought with exhaustion and fever.

"Oh, I'm so sorry. Um... I'll be right back," Kiko stuttered, hoping to fade into the background before rushing toward Tomi for aid. She overheard, instead, Kyoshi's mother tell Tomi, "Wattaan, tanmeen, miimanti kwimisoochi, kafuushi deebiru."

Neither Tomi nor Yuki planned to entertain Kiko today. They and the family were focused on the task at hand, removing all the torn paper from the screens, cleaning out all of the rooms, vacuuming the tatami, and clearing away any rotten foliage or brush surrounding the outdoor shrines. Kiko obliged. For several hours they scrubbed, dusted, and restored the home together.

Meanwhile, Tomi was setting up their altar room, which was made up of three shelves. The top held an ihai tablet of what looked like names with flowers on each side. The middle, or Nature God's shelf, was where she lit incense while muttering something in Uchinaaguchi under her breathe before placing it in the center aside the two cups, one with rice and the other with water.

Finally, she removed the items from her cart to place on the bottom shelf, which was already adorned with food offerings and gifts. Each person took turns rinsing off in the outdoor shower before dressing in clean clothes and returning indoors.

"Is it true?" Kyoshi whispered in Kiko's ear.

"Is what true?"

"Is she a yuta?"

"Is who a what?"

"Your obaa—is she a, you know, a witch?"

Kiko hesitated, at once afraid, confused, and excited. "Kachan? Why? Is that why we're here? I thought we were just helping you clean?"

"Well, I heard we were having a yuta come to cleanse the house and cure my great-grandfather."

Cleanse. Pray. This is what Yuki meant. So it is magic! Kiko nearly squealed with excitement before remembering this was not the appropriate time or place to do so. "Yeah, I remember hearing that word, but I don't speak, remember?"

"How do you not know if your own grandmother is a yuta? It's the most sacred position someone can hold around here. Do you know anything about your culture? Seriously?"

Kiko simply responded with "wow," stood up, and left. She couldn't believe he would say something so rude, and also so on point. She was learning, and she tried to learn more, but it wasn't her fault she didn't know about this stuff! Kiko was angry with her mom for not teaching her more, angry with herself for not learning faster, and even more upset that Tomi wouldn't say anything and let her look stupid like this in front of her only potential friend on this godforsaken island.

Kiko scoured the premises until she found Tomi in the garden with Yuki, waiting for the last of the family to come inside.

"Kachan!" Kiko shouted. "Are you a... a... a yuta?"

Tomi only smiled, her head tilted as if confused by the question.

"You know," Kiko pressed, "a witch?"

Still no response. In fact, Tomi's face was as blank as if she were pretending to have lost her hearing as well.

"Ugh! Forget it!" Kiko stomped on the ground. "I'm out. This is stupid anyway," she said, throwing a peace sign at the shocked faces of the family before trudging back home.

"So stupid!" she said, making sure Tomi was out of earshot. "All I did was ask a freaking question."

"Exactly," a scruffy voice said, seeming to come out of thin air.

Kiko spun around, trying to take in as much visual information as possible, but saw no one. She walked faster, wondering if it was a ghost. But hauntings only happen at night, right? No matter what Kiko told herself, she couldn't help but feel that she was not alone.

The house was empty, but it felt empty too, like energy was missing that wasn't before. A cold wind moved through the corridors and made Kiko shiver. She asked the breeze where it was when they needed it earlier, and a gust nearly knocked her over. What the hell was that? Kiko grew quiet and, with great apprehension, looked throughout the rest of the house before going to her room to read the articles she printed the other day.

"Don't believe everything you read," the voice called out again.

"Who's there?" Kiko shouted.

The silence was all that replied. Just as she closed her door and sooji screens, a sharp grip clutched her shoulder. Kiko screamed as she peered down at the dirty, elongated fingers with sharp talons that now stretched across her face, muffling her pleas for help. With great relief, she fanned out her fingertips and lifted them up as if to surrender to an arrest of some kind, or let him know she would be calm.

Soojimu smiled and released his grip before taking a seat on her bed, playfully juggling her phone and a few other items in between his hands.

"Wait. You speak English?" Kiko asked, perplexed by this notion.

"Aht!" Soojimu shook his finger. "I gave you the powers to understand Uchinaaguchi. Now, you won't struggle to understand your friend."

"Kyoshi? But he speaks English too."

"No, me! He may have brains, but he doesn't have centuries of mystical power," Soojimu hissed before returning to his playful demeanor.

"Of course, of course. I'm sorry. It's been a long day."

"I saw, your friend wasn't really a friend at all, was he? Very selfish and rude if you ask me. You were only trying to help."

"Right! You see that right? How come nobody else sees that!"

"I understand most certainly. People often mistake me trying to help as creating mischief when I am only trying to offer assistance. Others can be very ungrateful to people as kind as us," Soojimu said.

"I heard. But wait, don't you like that family? Kyoshi said that you are friends with his relatives?"

"Ah...We were friends once, yes. But they have forgotten me. Only his great-grandfather remembered to keep up our deal, but now that he is older, he has forgotten too. Now he's sick— it's really too bad."

"Wait—but you didn't make him sick, right?"

"Well, I didn't curse him, if that's what you mean. His own father did. We had an agreement, and friends don't fall back on their word. I was promised fresh fish and tea every evening so long as his family lives. I cannot help if they are punished for not being true to their promise. Right? Don't you agree?"

"But that's not what friends do."

"You're right! That is not what friends do! Friends don't forget friends! Right?" Soojimu shouted, vibrating the walls with his thundering voice.

"Right. But what I am saying is that he didn't forget you—at least not on purpose. He is sick. His memory is fading. In fact, Kyoshi said you are the only thing he remembers"

Soojimu's thick eyebrows furrowed as he leaned his neck side-to-side. "Ah, so this is why she is there," he said, pointing in the direction of the kitchen.

"Yes. I think she is supposed to be cleansing the bad juju in the house to cure him," Kiko nervously responded, hoping not to anger him again.

"Hmm," he grunted. "So you're telling me he never forgot me. He only forgets me now and then because of old age. Well, in that case, it is up to you to fix it. Tell his family I will forgive him, but only if they continue to honor his promise."

"But that wasn't his promise. It was his father's. Are you really going to hold that against them? Is that what your friendship means—to curse those who don't obey you?"

Soojimu laughed a bewildered, almost maniacal, laugh "Curse? Curse? Ask your grandmother about curses, not me. I only ask what was promised to me. They know what that means. Don't you worry. I hear everything at night. It's why I know who is pure of heart and who isn't. My very name means it, so I sense it everywhere I go, which is how I found you."

"Me?" Kiko asked. "But... I'm not pure of heart. I... I... You don't even know me! You have no idea what I have done or what I am capable of!"

His laughter only worsened. "Ahhh, but I do! I know who you are, Kiko. Your mother and I were good friends, and I sense her goodness within you. Listen, I will explain later. I know you're lonely and I will not always be able to keep your company because villagers have very nasty thoughts about me and will try to push us away from each other. To restore your faith in me, I will forgive him. Now, go on and tell the old man's family before your grandmother throws one of her fits," he said, pushing her toward the back door.

"Okay, okay! I got it!" Kiko said, but he was already gone.

Sprinting toward the house, Kiko felt confused between which one was which until she heard loud chanting in the distance. At the gate, an older man, in what appeared to be karate clothes, stopped her.

"I need to go inside!"

He shook his head and stood firm in his convictions to keep Kiko away from the house.

"Tell Kyoshi to tell his grandma that Soojimu will see his great grandfather tonight!" she said, hoping someone inside would hear her.

The name alone must have struck a chord with the guard because a look of shock washed over his face and, grabbing Kiko by the arm, he escorted her up the few steps and into the main foyer, where the family was gathered around the elderly figure, who lay under Tomi as she shook a white-tasseled object vigorously over him.

"Kachan! He is not sick. He is cursed!" Kiko shouted.

Everyone fell silent. Tomi all but breathed fire as her gaze pierced Kiko's very soul.

"Kiko—what do you mean?" Kyoshi asked.

"The kijimunaa, Soojimu. He told me to tell you that he will cure him as long as your family keeps their promise," Kiko said, using up all her breath.

Tomi, whether unphased or indifferent to this news, ignored it and continued to chant, shaking the tassels like maracas as she struck his limbs gently now and then. She then prepared an herbal tea, frothing it with a small wooden whisk, and fed it to the sick old man, who nuzzled it down like mother's milk before resting his head in Tomi's hands. Her tattoos seemed to change in color right in front of Kiko's eyes, as if a bolt of energy flowed through her hands, passed her fingertips, and into his mind.

Tomi chanted a bit more before completing the ritual and informing the family he would need rest. As Tomi spoke to the family, Kiko heard her name several times, even that of her mother's, and she grew frustrated trying to figure out what she was gossiping about and why she suddenly couldn't understand Uchinaaguchi again. That freakin' kijimunaa, brah. Kiko huffed, frustrated at her sudden linguistic disability after tasting the fleeting victory she felt only an hour ago.

Tomi picked up her materials and left without warning, leaving Yuki and Kiko to chase after her. Kiko knew this feeling well; she was being punished with silence. And Tomi, well, she had the coldest of shoulders. She had Mt. Fuji snow-cap shoulders, and any word or look that followed was bone-chilling and felt like frostbite.

Yuki would come into Kiko's room every now and then and drop an "ooh" with that "you're in trouble" tone as if they were still in school and someone was being called to the principal's office.

Finally, Kiko was so irritated, she slammed her door shut, closed all the sooji screens, and wallowed in the quiet humming that settled into the house, trying to focus on the light chirping of birds in the distance. She thought she might sleep, but all she could think about was her hunger and how she was too proud and ashamed to be near her grandmother right now. Still, she closed her eyes and tried.

"Kiko-chan, wake up." Soojimu's sing-songy voice echoed through the room as if each corner amplified it more than the last, until its melodic tune tap-danced on Kiko's ears. This, followed by a light tapping on the sooji screen, shifted her sleepy consciousness into that of an obedient subject, slugging toward the screen and opening it with what little energy she had left before throwing her body back onto the futon and shoving her face into the pillow.

"I brought you something," Soojimu said, holding out a shaved bark plate with fried snapper, rice, shaved daikon, and pickled vegetables. "I would have gone through the door to surprise you," he added. "But Tomi is a clever little cat of a woman. She left little wamon doku in front of each one tonight. I hope I didn't frighten you, friend."

"Wait, how come I can understand what you're saying in English, but then you still use words I don't know? What's wamon doku?"

"Well, I am a little rusty. I haven't made a friend here for many years, especially one who knew no Uchinaaguchi. But some words in our language just don't translate into words you'd understand in the language you speak."

"Oh, I see. And how come I can't understand anyone else who speaks it except you? And I can't speak it to anyone except you?"

"Well, Soojimu said, "how else would you appreciate something so ancient, so beautiful, if it were so easy to come upon? It wouldn't be fair to young Yuki, would it? If you were to just magically become all-knowing?"

"Well, I gue—"

"Guess what? That I am the trickster they make me out to be? The yanawarabaa? The mischievous, evil yuurii!"

"No…" mumbled Kiko. "It makes sense that I wouldn't understand. I have trouble learning things that's all. I thought it was really cool that we could talk, but when I went to warn Kyoshi, all that came out was stupid English!"

Soojimu pushed his gift of food closer, and Kiko began to eat listlessly.

"You want them to respect you. To accept you. I understand." Soojimu exhaled a deep sigh. "Uchinaaguchi is an oral language, not originally written. The great kami gave it to the people in music and song and spirit. It is felt just as much as it is heard, which is why it holds so much power. To give it to you, without you learning with your ears would be to deny your heart the strength and beauty it has. To learn, you must listen. You must try to speak."

Kiko knew what he meant. In fact, her mother would tell her the same thing when Yuki and Kiko argued or had a "misunderstanding," as she often called it. "So how come I haven't had dreams? What was it you gave me?"

"Good, huh? It's my own version of awamori, but for sleep. I have trouble too sometimes."

"Why is that?"

"Well I look young, but I am actually over 600 years old."

"What? Shibai! No way!"

Soojimu puffed out his chest proudly. "And I always looked like the youngest of the bunch too! My father was over 1,000 years old! His grandparents even knew the kami themselves!"

"Wha… You mean like…" Kiko pointed to the sky. "The gods?" she whispered as if she would be struck by lightning for saying it too loud.

Soojimu nodded boorishly. "You guessed it! And back then, your word meant something! Honor! Not like nowadays. I see so many in and out, every day, staring at that little magical block you always hold there. Never talk. Never listen. I imagine people do not care about each other anymore either! I thought it would be better after the disaster but more and more of the same."

"What disaster?" Kiko asked.

"Oh nothing. I merely came to bring you some food and offer good news. Kyoshi's great-grandfather will be just fine. Tomi did a fine job of healing him and removing the spirit that haunted the house. His first wife was always a bitter woman. Very jealous of our friendship, you know? Never liked me. When she died, I knew she would make it a point to make him pay for it eventually." He told Kiko his version of the story, how it was Soojimu who helped give Kyoshi's great-great-grandfather enough money to garner his future wife's attention and allow them to get married.

After a while, she grew jealous and hateful of their time together and burned down the banyan trees where he lived, hoping he was sleeping inside. But little did she know, he was spying on her all along. "Nobody can see us in the trees, but we can always see them," and that's when he cursed the wife, who, at the time, was with child—so he spared her death until the baby was born.

"See, I wouldn't kill a child. I have more mercy than she did. Humans have killed our kind for centuries, seeking out the gods or stealing our magic. I am the only one left here now. All the others went back to the other realm or elsewhere," he said somberly.

"Other realm?" Kiko asked in complete disbelief. "So like Harry Potter? Or Avatar: The Last Airbender? Or is it more like anime and Marvel, where it's completely two different worlds hidden on the same planet? I have so many questions."

"Slow down," Soojimu said. "I don't know what you're talking about."

"Wait. What? Ah, shucks well we should watch those then!" Kiko offered before remembering they had no wi-fi or cable. "Never mind. I forgot. We can't."

Soojimu didn't seem to mind at all. "I don't watch your theatre boxes. I enjoy live theatre myself, like an intellectual. It's those little things in your hands and in the human's faces all day, every day, that has the world messed up. It's no wonder they cannot remember their culture, their gods, their history—too distracted!" He pantomimed the large explosions in movies and guns used to kill people. "We know war, intimately. It is a life afforded by man, suffered by women, and endured by children. I don't need to watch it in my free time as the other yuurii do."

"Wait, what do you mean? There are more spirits here too?"

"Of course! What do you think happens in the afterlife? Especially now that people don't know how to properly bury their own Shimanchu and Uchinaanchu brothers and sisters? They remain stuck. So they haunt the family, old enemies, lovers, and so on. And nowadays they like to watch your movies, learn in your schools, and go to music festivals. They're learning more quickly than their ancestors, but what is the point if they cannot teach?"

"Mmm... I see. So, the ghosts, like the one Kachan banished, just kinda cruise 'em?" Kiko asked. She stretched out her arms and rested her palms on the back of her head as if about to lay down but instead moved her shoulders side to side, dancing.

"Yes! I used to follow people around like this as well, but in my old age, I have grown upset at the history people are being told, watching them repeat their ancestors' mistakes or witnessing the generations whitewash their heritage to embrace Western beliefs."

"Deep," Kiko said, finding it hard to really add much else. "I can't imagine what that was like."

"Awful," he said. "Each time and person, more hurtful than the last. Until I no longer wanted to be bothered by mortals and their petty grievances and quick-to-forget promises."

"I completely understand," agreed Kiko. "I've been betrayed a lot too. It makes it hard to make genuine friendships with people because someone else already hurt you, and even if they're not to blame, it's hard to trust them anyway." She reflected on her earlier treatment of Kyoshi, Tomi, and even her father.

"Yes. Very true. Well, I will let you get some sleep, Kiko-chan. If I remember correctly, Tomi will be leaving soon, and you both will be joining her. But don't worry I will watch over your house. Bring me something back, huh? A souvenir?"

Before she could ask what he meant, he vanished. She sighed with frustration, irritated that he always left before she could ask him a question. Somehow, whether it was just the length of the talk or the weariness from cleaning all day, she slept another dreamless night feeling the cool, island breeze rock her gently through the night.

The Guardian of Iriomote

Just as Soojimu predicted, Kiko woke up to clanking and stirring in the kitchen, but when she opened her eyes, it was still dark. She let out a deep yawn, stretched, and slowly mustered the strength to get up and see what was going on.

"What time is it?" she asked as she padded into the kitchen.

"Time to get a watch!" joked Yuki, spry as the sun that hadn't risen yet.

"Seriously, it's still dark out—what's going on?"

"I dunno. My shiisaa told me to wake up and help Kachan, so I did."

"Your what? Shiisaa? You mean the little things you made? Never mind," mumbled Kiko, struggling to stay awake while poking and prodding at her food.

Yuki, already bored, left the table to bother Tomi with several questions before coming back and telling Kiko to pack for a two-day trip. Remembering what Soojimu had said, she did so without any talking back or hesitation. In fact, she was rather excited to get off the island, packing her swimsuit, some extra clothes, and a journal to keep her company. Yuki, on the other hand, packed her toys and snacks, a few bits of clothes, but forgot to grab even the most basic hygienic necessities.

Fortunately, Tomi was a mother after all, and despite her apparent blindness, she was able to get around well and pack up everything else they'd need to survive on their journey, including the small shrine and its counterparts that she had brought to Kyoshi's. Kiko knew Tomi was worried because she heard her chanting using their names. Nevertheless, she rounded up all their belongings, organizing and reorganizing, until everything fit neatly into three small backpacks, one for each of them to carry.

Tutu does the same thing, Kiko thought, fondly remembering every field trip they prepared for, watching Tutu curse and swear while trying to get everything to fit in one bag, only to bring an extra purse and fanny pack as well. That said, Kiko was reminded to grab a small first-aid kit she left in her carry-on and pack that. "Cuz you can nevah be too careful, Tita," Tutu would say.

Mysteriously, there was already a water buffalo waiting outside to take them to the docks, and after a short clop, Tomi hopped into a seemingly random canoe that looked like a ferry from Greek mythology, with a lantern hanging over the bow like the one on the River Styx. Tomi encouraged the girls to join her, and with great apprehension, Kiko and Yuki stepped aboard, hand-in-hand. Tomi then unwound the loosely knotted rope at the pier's edge and, with a long oar, pushed away.

"Maa kai ichabiiga?" Yuki asked politely, looking toward the dark, early-morning sky.

"Iriomote," Tomi said quietly.

The girls never learned the time, but the sound of the waves splashing against the rocking boat and the thick sea mist wafting through the air made Yuki tired and Kiko nauseated. Tomi sang an old folk song about the lovers in the stars who can only meet once a year, or so Yuki translated. As they nodded in and out of sleep, Tomi would point to various stars and speak at length about their meaning and representation in Uchinaaguchi, but now that Yuki was asleep, Kiko had difficulty understanding, so she chose to listen with her heart instead. Tomi's voice was tranquil, making it easy to put the girls to sleep once she returned back to singing.

Kiko, resisting the urge to vomit, would doze in and out, peeping at Tomi as she was talking to herself and then chanting, until she noticed what she first thought was an aurora borealis flash in front of her. It wasn't that; in fact, it was much more amazing.

The ghostly bodies of women, men, and even children of all ages and periods, in various shades of smoky indigo and moonlight white, gathered above Tomi, who was chanting at the end of the boat. Then her chanting stopped, and every single pair of eyes turned to meet

Kiko's, including Tomi's, whose once milky eyes glowed like the rich turquoise Ryukyuan seas.

Slowly, Tomi turned her body toward Kiko. She lit a bit of incense, uttering what sounded like an incantation, then blew out the flame and the ash flew into Kiko's face, and she fell to the floor, forced asleep. Her mind would soon be floating, dancing between dream and reality. Each snapshot moment drifted seamlessly from one era of history to another. Except that she was no fly on the wall. Instead, she was seeing out of the bodies of those floating over her grandmother. And while she lived through their experiences, she could hear thousands of voices speaking from a thousand different corners of her mind, splintering her every waking thought.

As dawn broke, the sun's rays barely began to stretch over the glassy, placid water. It was enough light to sting Kiko's restless eyes. She was sick to her stomach and threw up over the edge. She apologized to the several manta rays beneath them, which didn't seem to notice as they gracefully glided through the open water. Tomi offered Kiko an onigiri, a small rice ball with umeboshi inside, and tea to ease her stomach. Squinting into the distance, Kiko could see the silhouette of an island, with large mangroves clinging to the shore, similar to those back home in Kāneʻohe bay.

But she had never seen one quite so stunning. As she stared at the clouds, she swore they looked like two shiisaa dogs meeting head-to-head in the center of the island, where the land cracked in half and offered a passageway into a cove. Tomi rowed inside, until they arrived at a narrow shoreline. With the flickering light showing the way, Kiko noticed a small spotted cat hiding in the trees and making its way down a branch toward them.

"Haitai, Yamamayaa," greeted Tomi, pulling a large frog out of her satchel and tossing it with great accuracy toward the cat's anticipating teeth. While the cat snacked on its treat, Tomi jumped into the calf-deep waters and pulled the canoe onto the sand. Kiko joined her, helping to secure the ties to the branches.

The splashing and shifting shook Yuki awake, who appeared rather surprised by their arrival. "We're already here?" echoed Yuki's shrill voice.

"*Shhh*," demanded Tomi, who nodded yes, pointing toward the mangroves and whispered, "Utaki" before she hauled the rucksack over

her shoulder and wiggled until it fit snug against her back. The girls did the same and copied Tomi as she slathered mud all over her arms and legs before heading inland behind the mysterious island cat.

For what felt like an eternity, the group trudged along a trail. Tomi foraged random plants as they suffered through steep inclines and muddy pits before following the river bed well into the island's rocky hilltops. Kiko loved hiking, but not today. She was overwhelmed and confused, hungry and tired. And to be honest, if they had to walk much further, she'd have preferred to give up and wait for Tomi's eventual return.

In truth, she wondered if Tomi's blindness made them lost, and why the hell they would trust a stray cat to guide them through the darkness? But that's when Kiko heard the rushing sounds of a stream hitting bedrock—a waterfall. Over-joyous that they were near one, Kiko felt rejuvenated and full of energy again. Yuki was already sprinting ahead, while Tomi took her time to meet them at the base of the plunge pool. Yuki tip-toed into the water, shrieking with delight at its fresh, cold sting, and Kiko joined in, splashing her face to cool herself off and jumping back at the shock of the cold as it trickled down her body.

Tomi let the girls play for a moment, before pointing behind the waterfall and waving them forward to follow her. Behind the curtain of rushing water was a deep cave that looked previously lived-in, with traces of a fire pit and a sleeping bag left behind. Tomi groaned as she stretched her weary muscles and laid down, insisting they do the same, before going into a deep sleep herself.

Kiko and Yuki pretended to sleep, like all children do, and waited until Tomi was snoring to go explore their surroundings a bit while the red sun broke through the trees and lit up the sky, illuminating a forest wonderland. Kiko began to contemplate what she might bring back for Soojimu. She knew he liked to fish, but it seemed he was already a great fisherman, yet he expected others to make him food. Before falling down another rabbit hole of thought, she rejoined Yuki at the pond, standing near its edge.

"Do you think Kachan comes here a lot?" Kiko asked. "I mean she had a sleeping bag and everything! And how doesn't she get lost?"

Yuki splashed her with water. "Why do you ask so many questions? Just enjoy the moment! I mean, how long has it been since we got to do this?"

"I know, but I mean that doesn't strike you as a little bit weird? I mean I know I am gonna sound crazy, but I swear I saw Kachan talking to ghosts this morning," Kiko muttered hesitantly.

"Oh yeah, for sure. I know that. My shiisaa told me so."

"Okay, what do you mean by that? Like, are you being serious or you're just trying to make fun of me?"

"Seriously! They told me she's a yuta and that we were going to prepare for the great harvest, and Kachan had to find ingredients from here. Ask them yourself!" Yuki said, pointing to the two small figurines on the large rock next to her clothes, remaining perfectly still.

Kiko got closer to the dogs, inspecting them as if she were a collector of sorts, until she brought them closer to her mouth and whispered, "can you hear me?" There was no response, and Kiko felt tricked.

Yuki loved pulling pranks, so of course, why wouldn't she do it now? But a howling sound caught her attention, as she gazed up at the small cat in astonishment. Do cats... howl? What is this place?

Kiko swore she saw the cat signal for them to return, so she called Yuki out of the water and they quickly dressed into their dry clothes and hurried up the short cliff, making it in perfect time to pretend they were still asleep as Tomi woke up.

Yuki, the actress, stretched and yawned as if she had a full night's rest. "Ukitan, Kachan!"

Tomi responded with a warm smile, as if not to wake Kiko.

But Kiko "woke up" anyway, thankful that Tomi didn't catch them outside playing when she insisted that they rest. Looking around for Yamamayaa, she spotted him at the heels of Tomi's feet and mouthed, "thank you." Tomi gently petted Yamamayaa before prepping a quick meal and heading out for their day's journey.

All in all, both the girls would soon regret not choosing to rest as the route ahead was long, arduous, and hot. The tea and simple meal of andansuu, a thick miso sauce with meat; 'nmu, steamed sweet potato; 'muu, a bright green algae knot; and rice, were hardly enough to keep them full all day. Mostly, the terrain was made up of pine trees, mangroves, and other brush that swept over the steep cliffs, but every once in a while, they came upon a bit of sugar cane, mango trees, and with each passing, Tomi collected leaves, fruit, seedlings, bark or branches while murmuring what sounded like a grocery list under her breath.

"Wuu-bingi," she said, pointing at the male mangroves, making a buzzing sound and slapping her forearm.

"Wuuji," she mentioned as she cut off its leaves with her hori-hori knife and snapped the cane to expose the sappy, sugary goodness while she danced, as if to indicate this helped with energy.

She went on like this for the entire trip, as Yuki translated and Kiko listened, repeating the words to herself, hoping it would stick in her memory. Kiko was rather proud of Yuki. Jealous, but proud, that she picked up their mother's native tongue so quickly and with such ease. Without Soojimu here, she appreciated knowing at least a little bit of what Tomi said. Sure, the body language and facial expressions helped, but she actually wanted to know what her grandmother was saying. She wanted to learn, and for that, she was thankful.

As the sun settled back into the spine of the mountaintop, Kiko felt some relief when they ended up at a beach. A brief moment of nostalgia swept over her as she recognized the bits of star-shaped sand that surrounded them. Mom kept these in a little jar by her butsudan, Kiko remembered fondly. Her mom would tell them the tales of Hoshizuna no Hama, the birth of star sand. However, it wasn't quite the same story being told by Tomi.

As Kiko remembered it, the story told of the North Star and Southern Cross, eager to give birth to their children in the Southern Loochoo Islands, where the water was calm and warm. But the stars never asked the Dragon God for permission, so he sent his serpent to swallow all the newborns and spit out their bodies across the shorelines as punishment.

But Tomi's version included a different perspective. She told us that after the Southern Cross gave birth, the stars fled back to the heavens, leaving their children to fend for themselves off of the Dragon God's resources.

When the Dragon God heard of the thousands of children left within his realm without his permission, expecting to live off of his wealth, he grew angry and felt disrespected. So he showered his shorelines with their dead bodies for the stars to see from above.

Witnessing this horror, the Southern Cross became plagued with grief. Her light dimmed, cursing seafarers who relied on her to navigate the open water. This also affected the Dragon God, whose sea trade now suffered from his own actions.

A powerful yuta, who claimed to hear the stars cry for their mother, devised a solution for both problems. She gathered the stars by the handful and brought them to an utaki. As she chanted, she burned the small stars with her incense and the smoke rose back toward the sky.

Day after day, one could see the small lights gather around the Southern Cross and shine brilliantly, finally reunited with her long-lost children.

"Ansukutu, wattaa ya kuma nkai wundoo," Tomi said, before continuing her story.

"She has to collect the star sand from this island because it is the last of them remaining, and they need to follow the... smoke... I think she said smoke... home," translated Yuki, as Tomi finished her story.

"Huh? Smoke?"

"One second," Yuki responded before clarifying with Tomi. "Yes, they burn the sand with the incense, and the smoke helps to guide them back to their parents. I guess she does this every year."

"Wow, that's incredible," said Kiko. "Are there more stories like this?"

Tomi nodded her head and said. "Uu." Yes.

As the night began to fall, Tomi made a small fire pit away from the shoreline and used it to cook what was left over from earlier, along with the new seaweed, limu, and fresh mangos from their adventures. For the remainder of the evening, Tomi told the girls all about the folklore on the island, as Yuki struggled to translate and Kiko attempted to absorb the stories' totality as best as she could, writing them down in her journal.

Tomi spoke of the Miruku and Saka, the competitive gods, who helped to cultivate the prosperous land of Okinawa, rich with animals, food, and festivals out of sheer spite for one another. Then she talked about the trees and the gods who made them, each with their own purpose and destiny. Then of the dog and princess, which reminded her of a spin on the Western princess and frog tale.

Every time Tomi finished one story, they begged for another, as children do when trying to avoid sleep or bound with excitement. Tomi continued to speak on the golden nuggets, the hidden underwater city, ghosts, and more until Yuki was curled up by the fire, mouth open and pouring out drool, clutching onto her shiisaa dogs, and Kiko was sprawled out, legs atop driftwood, nearly asleep.

Only then, Tomi resumed singing songs and packing away some of their belongings and unpacking others. She stacked bits and pieces of wood and wrapped them in banana leaves, until they took the shape of a small altar wherein she placed her ceramic dolls and stones and began to pray. Like before, spirits sprang up from the sand, and their half-illuminated bodies encircled Tomi like sharks. Kiko couldn't help but hear them, and it was the hushed shouts and whispers that woke her up.

Her once anchored eyelids attempted to force themselves open in long, slow blinks, as if gathering enough moisture to glide up and down with their usual ease, until she found herself staring at the ghosts, who were staring back at her. Not again. You're dreaming. This is a dream. Kiko shook her head violently hoping that they would disappear, but they wouldn't. Instead, they began to speak more and in archaic tones she didn't comprehend.

Until one ghost, whose voice she recognized instantly, commented, "Anmaa, just tell her the truth." Tomi, along with all the spirits, nodded in agreement. Her milky eyes swirled like smoky glass balls that foretold fortunes, and slowly, she turned back to Kiko, who stared in awe and confusion.

Then it hit her: that voice—Mom! Kiko shot up with such fervor, it felt as though she had drunk several energy drinks or had been brought back to life by way of electrocution.

"Mom? Mom!" Kiko shouted, running headfirst at the gathering of spirits.

But they all disappeared as Kiko approached. "Bring her back, Kachan! I said bring her back!"

Tears welled up her eyes and streamed down the sides of her face. "Please, Kachan. Please!" Kiko pulled and begged at her feet, but Tomi did not move.

Tomi only said, "No." Kiko couldn't tell if this was Okinawan for something else or if she was speaking English for the first time, but a fury-like tornado whirled within her at the mere utterance of the word.

Kiko walked over to Yuki and shook her awake, pulling her up and demanding they leave now.

"What... what happened?" Yuki cried out.

"Kachan is crazy! A witch! She has our mom, and she took her away before I could see her! We need to leave before she does something to us!

I will explain later!" Kiko shouted, each statement with more emphasis than the last

Yuki stared down Tomi, who was sitting peacefully by the flames and waving them goodbye, before grabbing her shiisaa dogs and quickly following Kiko who was already leaps and bounds ahead.

"Wait for me! Kiko, wait!"

Kiko's anger fueled her movements, and she tripped countless times and cursed at everything that got in her way.

"Kiko, they said this is dangerous. We should go back," hinted Yuki, holding up her shiisaa.

"You tell your dogs to shut up. I know what I'm doing!" Kiko snapped. Just then, Kiko felt the cold sting of water as she tumbled into the river and began coursing along with the current. Her head bobbed in and out of the water as she struggled to breath, and she watched helplessly as a panicked Yuki jumped in after her. But as Yuki got closer and closer, she looked more and more afraid, and at the sound of another splash in the distance, a frightened Yuki jumped onto Kiko's shoulders and accidentally pushed her under in an attempt to stay afloat. The brackish water rushed into Kiko's ears, nose, eyes, and mouth, and just like that, Kiko was reliving the very moments that she tried so desperately to forget. Only this time, nobody was there to save them. She was sure they would die, and it would be all her fault.

Yamamayaa

Bruised, battered, and beaten, Yuki woke up back at the cave. The cascading waterfall reflected the moonlight, and the pins-and-needles feeling throughout her body reminded her that she was alive after all. Yuki sat up, startled, making sure Kiko was alive too, only to find her in the arms of Tomi, who seemed to be stitching up her head.

"Get away from her!" demanded Yuki.

"Shhh, Yuki-chan," hushed Tomi, gently nudging away Yamamayaa, who was licking the blood from Kiko's head wounds.

Tomi pushed a small bowl of blackish paste toward Yuki.

"Kuree nuu yaibiiga?" Yuki asked, curious to know what it was but naturally began to place it over her wounds as she noticed it all over Kiko's torn up body. It looked to be made of mangrove leaves, mud, and some kind of sticky sap that stuck to her raw skin, forcing her to yelp now and then while applying it, trying to remember what happened.

"Is she gonna be okay? Please tell me she's going to be okay. I can't... I can't lose her too, Kachan," Yuki sobbed. It was as if her mother's death finally hit her, and the fear of being alone was becoming too much to bear.

But Tomi didn't respond. She just continued to chant over Kiko's pale and bloody body, rocking it back and forth in her lap. Yuki could tell Tomi was crying by the glistening trails on her face and decided to mimic her chanting beside her. The fire crackled loudly as the pot boiled over, and Tomi instructed Yuki to remove it carefully and bring a small cup to her, so she may give it to Kiko.

As it cooled, Yuki did her best not to hurl at the smell, which reminded her of the small, black Chinese medicine balls in orange and brown glass jar their mom would give them for stomach aches. Wincing at the cup, she reluctantly handed it to Tomi, whose fingers were wrapped around Kiko's chin, forcing it open and pouring it in. Immediately, Kiko's eyes shot open, and she began to cough up phlegm, water, and bits of moss and algae, while crying out in pain. Every minute or so, this would continue until Kiko was too weak to hold her body up any longer, falling back into Tomi's lap.

Tomi wanted to ensure she didn't fall asleep, since she had a bleeding, baseball-sized lump stitched closed on her head. So now and then, she would shake her awake and administer more of the liquid concoction. Every time, Kiko would throw up more of the same things, until she finally grew so hungry, her mouth so wrought and dry with bitter stomach acid, she could only say "food."

She gathered all the strength she could manifest and used it to hoist herself up to a seated position, causing Yuki to bounce up and down with joy. Kiko hardly noticed; in fact, she was so weary, all she could think about was the water trapped in her ears. She was annoyed that her short, stubby fingers couldn't reach far enough to release it.

"Ugh, I feel like shit," Kiko managed to say. "What was in that tea, or whatever it was?"

"A bunch of stuff. I dunno. So, I know it's bad timing, but you owe me a dollar for using a bad word," snickered Yuki.

Kiko ignored her and continued to moan and groan, as Tomi stood over the pot, stirring in their leftover rice and some packets of ochazuke until it thickened into a porridge.

Kiko and Yuki ate so quickly, they hahafafafa'd past the boiling hot sensation and swallowed without much chewing until the pot was scraped of all its contents.

Finally, looking around, Kiko wondered how they got back to the cave when it took a whole day just to get to the other side. She wondered how much time had passed and who had saved them. It hurt to think, but it was inescapable. Reaching up to her temple, she felt the lumps from the stitching and continued to shape her hand around the large, swollen lump, worried that she now looked freakish and deformed.

Then out of the corner of her eye, Kiko noticed the brown-spotted cat with yellow eyes that seemed to glare at her.

Actually, she noticed several Iriomote cats, and when she finally turned her head, she realized there were over a hundred in the cave, all quietly resting around them. Out of curiosity and a small hint of worry, she asked Yuki how long they had been there. Yuki didn't know either, as she was just beginning to see them amass herself. Kiko began scooting her body closer to Yuki until they were nearly back-to-back, both gazing at the large gathering with alarm.

Each cat began stretching out their limbs and made their way toward one another, some leaping from carved ledges in the cave, stacking on top of one another until they morphed into one large, twenty-foot tall cat that purred gracefully under Tomi's drawn out tattooed fingertips, as if adhering to the arrow-like markings in a *come hither* signal.

"This," Tomi said with a grin, "is Yamamayaa, the Guardian of Iriomote."

Tales of the Yuta

Kiko and Yuki gaped at Yamamayaa with such shock that their jaws nearly stretched to the floor. The once cute, cuddly kitten was now a large, menacing predator with teeth longer than their arms or legs, and talons sharper than the finest katana blades.

"B-b-but how?" stuttered Kiko, too disturbed to put to words what she was seeing.

"Well," Yamamayaa declared. "How else could I look over an entire island myself?"

Kiko heard heavy growling behind her and turned to see Yuki shaking, the front of her pants wet.

"Tell your dogs to heel, child. They are far too young to stand against me," Yamamayaa said to Yuki, who hushed the two little figurines beside her.

Kiko had no clue why Yamamayaa would worry about two small clay dogs, but she couldn't find the source of the growling either. "Wait, are you saying her shiisaa are real?"

Yamamayaa and Tomi shared a hearty laugh. "Yes, Kiko," Tomi said. "All shiisaa are real. Who do you think warned me to save you? They are guardians too, after all."

This was becoming too much, too soon for Kiko, who had to wonder if she was still asleep, or even possibly dead, as ways to explain all of this.

"I told you," Yuki boasted proudly.

"Wait. Now suddenly you speak English, Kachan? Unless... Is Soojimu here?"

"Soojimu!" Yamamayaa cried out, laughing so loudly it shook the cave. "Soojimu would not dare come to my island!"

"I understand everything," Tomi interrupted. "I am one with every language, as you are. We only pretend not to be when it proves to our advantage. Soojimu and Yamamayaa are not friendly with one another —a centuries-long hostility between them," she added.

"And for centuries to continue!" hissed Yamamayaa.

"But why?" asked Kiko. "And you just watched us struggle to guess what you were saying out of pure entertainment? You're not even blind, are you?"

Letting out a brief chuckle, she responded, "Well, at my age, you have to have fun however you can. Plus, no good not to speak your mother tongue, as they say, nmarijima nu kutuba wasshii."

"Nee kuni n wasshiin," the girls joined her in unison.

"That's right, to forget your native tongue means to forget your native country, your people, and your history. It is a dying language, you know. You should thank me for making you learn what your mother should have taught you!"

"So, you're not blind either?" Yuki asked her again, ready to throw a fit.

"I never said I was blind. You only assumed I was."

Yamamayaa roared with laughter, rolling onto her back and kicking her large paws into the air.

"But my eyes," Tomi continued. "Well, they say it's a family curse. Only happens every once in a while, only to women. Before the Japanese took over, it was a blessing. It meant you were destined to be a yuta. Before, my eyes looked very much like Kiko's: green like the gajumaru around us, with hints of sky and fire as well. Our eyes are elemental; they change as we feel different emotions, but after the war... Well, let's just say it became very difficult to feel again after seeing so much."

"So much what?" Yuki asked.

"Death, Yuki. She means death," blurted Kiko.

"Yes, the Battle of Okinawa scars this land in more ways than one. The Japanese and Americans fought over our land and killed many of us in the process. I was only a girl, fourteen, when the war started, and the girls in our school were asked to become nurses. We were called Himeyuri Corps, over two hundred girls and only four of us remained after the war," Tomi managed to say before choking on tears.

"Your grandmother was stunning in battle," purred Yamamayaa. "I have never seen anything like those girls in all my time. Tomi caught my attention because she rendered aid even in the most dangerous of terrains. I would follow her as she dragged the children with missing limbs or bullet-ridden bodies back to their cave, hiding underneath dead ones at the sounds of oncoming American or Japanese troops. They were tactless. Killed on sight. Okinawan, Japanese, they didn't care—all that mattered were the numbers, and that's all we were in their eyes."

"We had very little to sustain us," continued Tomi. "We had to rely on the things around us. The mangrove could be used as an astringent, fire sanitized our minimal surgical tools, and we had the patients bite on bark from trees to stifle their screams while we performed amputations. The same chopsticks we used to eat, we used to pick out the maggots from our wounds and the wounds of others. We were afraid; some of my closest friends killed themselves to avoid being taken by American soldiers. I almost did too, until I met Yamamayaa."

Tomi continued to pet the giant cat who stretched across the length of the cave, purring at her touch. She went on to tell the girls about the gas attacks and how they were instructed to urinate on their pants and hold it against their mouths if they wanted to survive. Yuki, no longer embarrassed at having an accident earlier, asked to hear more. Yamamayaa and Tomi took turns detailing the war, like two friends talking about the good ol' times. But this wasn't that. Instead, it was how the Imperial Army forced the yutas to go to "normal school," to heal the wounded, and to curse the enemy, or even their own people, with black magic. Because many refused, they were shot and killed. Tomi only survived because Yamamayaa approached her, rubbing against her leg, as she was prepared to jump off a cliff.

This small act of kindness from the wounded kitten changed the outcome of Tomi's life. She cared for her, sharing her own small rations of food, until she became stronger. Until eventually Yamamayaa yielded enough strength to return to her full form.

"Ikusa ndi, duu ya ipuu mutchootin, eeti ru yanamun yasa," sneered Yamamayaa at Tomi.

"Huh?" Kiko shook her head trying to discern fragments of the what they were saying.

"In war, the other person is always the bad guy—even if it is only you holding the gun," Kachan warned.

"It was the Iron Dragon," Yamamayaa said. "He lives for war; it fuels him. Each death brings him strength, and though he is larger than any whale and longer than any rope, he can shrink to the size of the smallest lizard, so that he may whisper and manipulate others to do his bidding. But your grandmother would not let him get away with it. Together, we and the boy who would become your grandfather defeated the Iron Dragon. For a small price that is." He revealed a large, lightning-storm scar branching out over his stomach.

Tomi furrowed her brow. "They never recovered the Iron Dragon's body. But after the damage was done, we had to make sure Yamamayaa would live. I took her back to the cave and healed her. It took many nights and the strength of all my power to do so. She barely clung onto life. When the war was over, I promised to bring her back home so that she could care over what little villagers she had left. Then, I stole a small riverboat and brought her here."

"We gather every year around this time, in this space, to eat, play and hunt—so we may never forget what it took to survive those long months," added Yamamayaa. "But nowadays, she can barely lift herself up, huh Tomi-chan? And when the shiisaa came, I knew I had to return the favor."

Tomi laughed. "Don't listen to her. In a fight, I would still win." She added sticks to the fire to boil more tea.

Kiko was a bit overwhelmed with this mythical lore and horrifying realizations. "What did those things mean by 'tell her the truth'? Was that really my mom?" she asked.

"Another day," Tomi stated. "And those *things* are your ancestors—show some respect."

"I'm sorry, I just…" Kiko could feel a lump form at the back of her throat as she struggled to respond. "I just have so many questions…"

"You sure do," Yamamayaa said. "I was surprised you stayed quiet enough to hear the story." She chuckled, curling around Tomi's aged and weary body.

Kiko folded her arms across her chest. There was an energy growing inside her, nearly boiling over, and tears began to run down her cheeks. "I know, I know, and I'm sorry. I just… I'm sorry, Kachan. I know I killed her! It was me! It was me, and I don't deserve to be here! It should have been me! I was meant to die! And I should have died in the river tonight, and she should have let me!"

Tomi exhaled deeply as if she were unsure how to respond or comfort her. She opened her arms, inviting Kiko in for the first time, and hugged her tightly. Eventually, the tears stopped and breathing slowed.

"Ah, Kiko-chan. Mii ya tin niru aru—our fates are as registered by the heavens," Tomi whispered gently. "You are no murderer. You are only guilty of surviving such a horrible event, and sometimes, that is a fate worse than death. I know," she said, holding Kiko to her chest.

"I'm so sorry," whimpered Kiko.

"Shh, shh, shh," soothed Tomi, continuing to rock her back and forth, as Kiko took long and heavy breaths.

Finally, Kiko felt herself drifting to asleep, and with Tomi alongside her, Yamamayaa stretched the way kittens do, extending her arms out to Yuki and her shiisaa dogs, wrapping around all of them as the kindling fire slowly turned to ash.

The Journey Back

The morning sun snuck in later than the days before. Perhaps, just like the group, it needed a bit more time today. Well, at least most of the group. Tomi was washing their clothes, littered with blood, mud, and gods-know-what. Yuki, short and spry, leaped to her feet almost as soon as her eyes opened. Upon seeing only a small cat curled up where the once large beast laid and Tomi nowhere in sight, she jogged down the path to join her grandmother.

"Good morning, Kachan!" Yuki called out, quickening her pace.

Tomi cleared her throat loudly, as if demanding some sort of correction in Yuki's behavior, bringing her to a total halt.

"Wassaibiin, Kachan. Ukimisoochii," Yuki said, trying to maintain a cheerful disposition.

"Mii iraa, kubi wuuriri," Tomi scolded.

Yuki hated being scolded, especially when she couldn't say anything back. But she was going to prove to Tomi she wasn't lazy at all, and she was certainly not going to let her honor fall by the wayside, whatever that meant. Struggling to come to grips with her temper, Yuki decided to turn to her cute and playful self because "nobody can say no to cuteness."

Of course, like everyone else, Tomi too submitted.

Her harsh tone soon withered away, and she began singing the same old tunes they knew and loved with soft melodic tones. Kiko was still too weak from the night's injuries to hold herself up too long, so she stayed in the cool, dry cave enjoying the peace and quiet, as well as the rather pleasant company of Yamamayaa. Kiko could hear Yuki's tone-deaf singing outside, which she felt even the nicest people had difficulty listening to, and she let out an exasperated sigh.

She couldn't believe everything that happened, all the stories they told her, and the idea that the stories might actually be true. And wow, Yamamayaa must be old to have seen all that. Like really old, like hundreds of years old!

Thoughts and questions paraded through Kiko's mind until they riddled her with a migraine. She wondered if Tomi had put a spell on her so that every time she thought about it, she'd experience pain. That's what Kiko would do if she wanted someone to shut up, and it only furthered her suspicions.

Footsteps echoed through the cave as Tomi and Yuki returned.

"Haitai, Kiko-chan," said a smiling Tomi, whose head tilted in a way that made her appear like a curious child.

"Haitai, Kachan," Kiko responded.

"Today, some good friends of mine are going to take us to a very special place," Tomi announced. "We will use today to relax and eat before leaving tonight."

Kiko let out a long, painful moan. "I don't think I am strong enough, Kachan. Everything hurts."

"You will be fine soon. The tea will cure you. Your cuts are already gone, and the bump has subsided. I know it doesn't taste good, but good medicine never does," Tomi said, refusing to take no for an answer.

Kiko soon realized she was telling the truth. Her bump felt only like a small pebble or pimple, and as if by a miracle, under the T-shirt bandages Tomi wrapped her in there was no blood, only a thin veil of mud covering her skin. Kiko limped toward the waterfall, using the mist to wash away the dirt and stood in shock. Suddenly, she felt no illness at all, standing tall and walking back like a new person.

"You are not done healing," Tomi reminded her. "The tea will help until we reach our destination. It won't take long since we have friends to guide us."

"Why don't we take the boat back?" Kiko asked.

"Well, silly girl, you tied the boat to a branch, and when the high tide came in, it washed away. Who knows where it is by now," Tomi said with a laugh.

Kiko felt red in the face. She couldn't believe she didn't consider that. Especially since she had gone on so many canoes and always helped anchor them back home. Kiko didn't know why Tomi laughed instead of yelling at her, and the nervousness made her skin itch.

"It's just a boat. Now relax, and trust me when I say we have a better ride," Tomi said tenderly.

"I am so sorry," apologized Kiko. "I should have known better."

"Kiko-chan, it is okay! You will only be sorry if you continue to feel sorry, instead of being present."

Kiko wasn't used to being forgiven like this. Maybe she has more boats? Maybe it wasn't hers to begin with. Back home, if this had happened, she would have caught lickings for doing something so foolish. Tutu had zero tolerance for "one half-assed job," and since their mother didn't believe in physical punishment, she let Tutu handle that instead. "It takes a village" was often what they would catch their mother saying after getting spanked by Tutu's leathery palm, rice paddle, or nearby slipper. But now, nothing. Tomi laughed, and that confused Kiko in a way that only made her smile.

Tomi wasn't joking when she said she had a better ride lined up for them because as they approached the shoreline, Kiko spotted the manta rays relaxing in the bay. Shooting her head back and forth between Tomi, Yuki, and the water, Kiko grew more and more excited.

As they gathered closer to the shore, Kiko felt only slightly hesitant to go in. She didn't know whether it was due to her excitement because she'd always wanted to swim with rays or because she felt safe knowing that her grandmother was there too. Fast approaching were three large-winged jet-black manta rays, and Yuki squealed with excitement before hopping to remove her shoes and dress down to her bathing suit.

Tomi greeted each one as if they had been long time friends, and they lifted their wings to embrace her. She gave the girls instructions on how to approach them. "Treat them as you would gods. Do not demand. Do not push. Only listen and obey what they ask you to do." Though Kiko didn't know what this actually meant, she was stoked to give it a shot.

Tomi invited Yuki first, and, as with everything else, she took to ray-riding with great ease, gracefully switching between water and air.

"Okay, Kiko, this may be difficult because it requires you to breathe underwater. They will teach you how if you listen. But to listen, you must be calm and remain open. Do you understand?" Tomi asked firmly.

"Yes, I'll do my best."

"No, there is no doing your best. You do, or you don't do. That is it," Tomi said, her hand cutting through the air like a knife. "Follow me."

Kiko followed her, taking long deep breaths, which seemed to actually work. By the time she realized how calm she was, the ray was already caressing her with its large, slick wings. Kiko found herself atop one of the most beautiful creatures she had ever seen, and Tomi was right: something about this felt rather regal as they moved with such poise through the sea.

As they passed an array of small, skipping-stone sort of islands, they could see Taketomi from afar but seemed to be headed in a different direction. The girls didn't mind as they enjoyed the freedom of breathing underwater and watching all the sea creatures passing by: a small whale shark the size of *DaBus*, schools of different fish traveling to colorful coral reefs, and few different boat wreckages, which reminded Kiko of their own boat lost to the tide. Such trivial thoughts subsided when they arrived at Kuroshima island, better known as "black island, "heart island," or "land of cows."

The manta rays spoke with a smooth eeriness in their voice, like that of sirens or other profound beings, and Kiko could swear she heard them gossiping about Tomi and whether or not "she could tell her" something. Who "she" was, Kiko had no clue, but she rested her ear on the back of the ray and gleefully listened to them continue. She remembered how much she enjoyed the ocean and the world within it before the incident. A deep longing for Hawai'i, Tutu, La'akea, and her friends at school washed over her, and a small piece of her felt sad that she could so easily forget about them. Suddenly, being in the water only reminded her how different it was from back home.

Diving deep into the turquoise waters of Kuroshima, the rays glided playfully, rolling and zooming now and then to show off their skills. When they breached the surface, they ended up in another cave. This one looked as though it had the glow-in-the-dark stars they once had in their rooms back home. But these were no stars; they were small glow worms gathering in tiny colonies throughout the cavern, illuminating large stalagmites towering over them.

Tomi and the girls thanked the rays for safely bringing them here and stepped onto the rocky terrain. The rays then floated peacefully in the water as if awaiting the group's return. Tomi escorted the girls to the back with nothing but the glowworms to light their path. They ended up in the depths of the cavern, staring up at large paintings on the walls.

"You see, this is our family legacy," Tomi said. "Before we were colonized by Japan, our family was very well to do. In fact, your grandfather's family came from a long line of royalty."

Yuki yelped with joy. "Wait, are you saying we're royal too?"

"No. Well kind of. His family were noros, head priestesses, to the royal family. Sometimes, they are same-same, but other times not so much. His family was the loyal retainers, so it was only natural that he and I would be drawn to one another. See this large painting of the castle? That's where our families stayed. Most of our history is empowered by women—not so much now. Naichaa men did not like women to be in power; they like women to be silent, obedient, and submissive. So many years of oppression and people forgot their strength." Tomi sighed.

As she pointed to each fragment of the illustrations, she explained the process of becoming a yuta and how they were seen over time. In the beginning, the noro and yuta were sisters. First, they were the kaminchu, spiritual mediums, helping with rituals, ceremonies, cleansings (much like the one they performed at Kyoshi's), and blessings of the harvest.

The yuta could see and feel ancestral spirits, while the noro could see the gods in any form, whether it was clouds, water, animals, so on and so forth. The yuta were most similar to kaminchu, drawn to spirits all around them, similar to what Kiko saw earlier, and the noro were surrounded by natural elements and animals.

Following the drawings, Tomi explained the history of the practitioners, and how, over time, the Japanese imperial forces and Chinese began to banish the shamans to other islands in fear they may be cursed by them. They saw the villagers with torches chasing them down and setting their homes on fire while they slept. They saw the dragon, followed by what appeared to be famines, volcanic eruptions, tidal waves, a large explosion, and then at the very end, a small girl wrapped in an orb entangled with another dragon.

"Who is that?" Yuki pointed indiscreetly.

"This, Kiko, is what we need to talk about," Tomi stated.

"What do you mean? Why?" Kiko stammered, seemingly confused by her proclamation.

"Because this girl... is you. This is your destiny. The truth I have been waiting to unfold."

Everyone stood still. So still, they could hear the water dripping from the limestone as it plopped into the inch-deep water that flowed beneath them. "That's not fair! Why does she get to play with a dragon?" Yuki asked.

"She is not playing, Yuki-chan. This is not the time for petty games. Kiko, this is much, I know. But it is why I brought you here. I know you have so many questions, but I am sure this is you. Before, I thought, maybe your mom, maybe one of my other children, but they lost their way. I could feel it was you the moment you set foot onto Taketomi. I watched you as you got off the boat—powerful energy around you, very powerful." Tomi paused, looking concerned. "I didn't want to worry Yamamayaa, but I am afraid the Iron Dragon is back. In fact, I am certain he is the one that dragged my Sako to her death."

Kiko's heart sank, because she knew somehow it all had to be connected. She could only ask but a single question, containing a single word.

"Mom?"

Wishing Upon the Stars
(Kiko)

What do you say when someone tells you that you are destined for a battle that you are not sure you can win? What was I supposed to say when my grandmother, who until now I assumed was blind and knew no other language than Uchinaaguchi, tells me I am a yuta? That I, in all my four feet and ten inches, am going to fight something called Iron Dragon? Like seriously? Don't get me wrong, the possibilities are amazing, but this wasn't what I was hoping for. I wanted it to be like the books I read, or the shows I watched—key word here being *watched*. Not like this. I don't want to actually be the hero. And as much as I've thought about it, I didn't want to die either.

I couldn't help but just stare at Kachan blankly as she just dropped some big facts and expected to hear some answers. I didn't have any. I had more questions if anything, but I didn't know how to translate my thoughts into questions. All I could think about was her saying, "I am certain he is the one that dragged my Sako to her death."

All of a sudden, my world was upside down. If my mind were a computer, it'd have a bunch of tabs open like, "Found out I can talk to ghosts, what now?" and "How to become a yuta," and "Communicating with the Dead for Dummies" and of course, "What to say to your mom who you thought you killed but was killed by someone else who I coincidently now have to fight to avenge her death and restore my family's honor?" I felt myself getting dizzy. Who am I, Prince Zuko? Is this my character arc? Really? What else is there? Do I also have to worry about his mafia of steel lizards or other metal-themed reptilians? Would I defeat the evil forces with my handful of years of karate? My head was pounding with questions, demanding answers, but it felt more like I had banged it against a wall several times instead.

Meanwhile, fragments of what Kachan was saying involving my training (kamis, kaminchu, sanjinso, and yutas, among other things) were making me weary. Honestly, I was just so hungry, I couldn't think anymore. I didn't remember when we last ate, and suddenly it was all I could focus on. Because in the last seventy-two hours, I nearly drowned, saw dead people, met a twenty-foot cat, swam with manta rays, and learned I came from a family of magical shamans and royalty. It was all becoming too much for me to handle.

"I am sorry. This is just a lot, and I am just really tired. I would just like to go home, please. When are we going to go home?" I asked Kachan, hoping she would hear the sincerity in my voice.

I really did want to go home. I just wanted to lie down on that bumpy futon and eat some chips and ice cream or something, and go to sleep. I knew that would be impossible but honestly, I would rather read prodigal epics than be in one right now.

I saw the disappointment in her face as she told me we had one more thing to do before we returned home, and she led us back toward the rays. Her silence was deafening, and she refused to meet my eyes as we prepared to leave. I knew I should have said more, but what did she expect from me? I wasn't ready for this news; I was barely ready for puberty! I felt like everyone was mad at me for not sharing their excitement.

Even the rays' earlier chirping quieted down as I watched the coral reef pass by more quickly. I could tell they were displeased with me too. The moment we arrived back on the shore of Taketomi, the ray I rode upon left quickly, with no goodbye wave as the others had given to Yuki and Kachan. I felt sick to my stomach. Everyone was expecting me to just jump in the air and leap with joy at the fact I may very well be killed, and this beast who killed my mom would somehow succumb to me, and it was just unfair. Nobody knew what I was dealing with. Of course, I wanted to defeat the dragon, but I just didn't know how. I could barely gather the courage to swim in the water, let alone fight within it.

But for now, we were safely back on the shore. I looked forward to talking to Soojimu about everything that happened and get his insight as to what I was supposed to do. Maybe see what he knows about this Iron Dragon fiasco. Then the pit in my stomach returned. I forgot to get him a souvenir.

"Crap," I muttered.

"What?" Yuki replied, still clearly annoyed.

"I forgot to get something. A souvenir from our trip. Kachan, do you happen to have something small I can give to a friend?" I asked.

She still wasn't speaking to me. Instead, she continued walking further down the shoreline, and I could only barely see her figure crouching over her small alter, lighting up incense.

"Kachan?" I asked again.

"Shut up, Kiko!" Yuki shot back. "Don't you see she's busy? Do you only think about yourself?"

My face fell flat, and I couldn't seem to look up from the sand sticking to the little hairs on my toes. I wasn't thinking of myself. I was worried about what Soojimu might do if I didn't bring him something back. But she was right. I sounded selfish, and the only thing I could do was just stand here, shut up, and let Kachan do her thing.

I crept up slowly, trying not to make too much noise as I heard her praying over the incense, pouring a small vial of the star sand over it. I listened carefully to the rhythm of her prayer, its cadence, the words, and did my best to mimic her as I knelt aside her. I figured maybe if I prayed with her, she would acknowledge my existence, but she simply put up two fingers and dragged them across the air towards me as if to say "stop." I was irritated because she just told me this was my legacy, and now that I was trying, she was telling me to stop?

But before I knew it, I saw why. An airy blue mist rose from the ashes of the incense, and I watched it trail across the sky and shoot into the backs of the manta rays. Their backs began to glow like Kachan's hajichi, and their small dots and stripes shone ever so clearly underneath the night sky. Only, this wasn't the end of it.

As I peered into the water, their bodies began to disfigure. The lobes that safeguarded their mouths began to take the shape of ears, their wings began to stretch into thin drawn-out arms, their eyes growing closer together, while their fins elongated like a spine and legs sprang up beneath them. They were shapeshifting into human figures: a tall slender man in fine robes with long straight hair, an equally tall woman dressed in all white robes which draped against the open water, and a ghostly figure of a child with no face, genderless and naked.

As if I couldn't possibly comprehend anymore, I just stood in shock. I looked over to Yuki, who was gawking at the child. "Don't stare, Yuki!" I whispered loudly.

"My shiisaa told me they're gods."

"Gods? You mean to tell me we were riding on the backs of gods?"

"Shh!" hushed Yuki. "I am trying to listen!"

So I waited. I watched as the illuminated figures stood out in the waters and embraced each other, then opened their arms to welcome the child. Before I knew it, their bodies shot into the sky, and the stars began to twinkle much more vibrantly. As we watched, a pleasant sprinkling of rain began to fall.

A blessing from the Gods, I thought. Finally, Tutu's words became clear and I began to wonder if maybe, back home, all of this exists too. If La'akea's stories about Hawaiian mythology weren't stories at all—that maybe all of the things we were told didn't actually exist were real.

Dreams and Nightmares

Though Kiko basked in the amazement of seeing the ancient gods and her mother's story of the star sand come to life in the last forty-eight hours, it would end with a quiet return to Tomi's home, which looked a bit more ominous than it had before. The crescent moon hung low over the roof, and not even a breeze drifted by to cool or dry them as they approached, still soaking wet from their earlier escapades.

Kiko and Yuki were teeming with questions, but Tomi's silence made it clear that they would have nobody to ask, especially her. She returned to her prayer room, restored the altar to its simple beauty, then headed to the kitchen to prepare some miso soup, eggs, and rice for the girls before leaving for her room. Not knowing whether she was upset or tired, Kiko and Yuki ate quietly, only exchanging brief, excited whispers over what they had just seen.

"That was the coolest thing ever," Yuki said. "I mean did you see how fast they shot up to the sky? It was like shooting stars but... I dunno... opposite!"

"It's like I close my eyes, and I see it all over again. Hey, you think she's still mad at me?" Kiko nodded toward Tomi's room.

"She's probably just tired. That looked like it took a lot out of her, and not everything is about you, you know?"

"I wasn't saying that! Ugh. Never mind, forget it." Kiko sneered, stood up from the chabudai, and walked away.

"Hey! You might be a yuta or whatever, but if you think I'm doing your dishes, you're crazy!" Yuki snapped.

124

With a frustrated grunt, Kiko grabbed her dishes and washed them loudly and furiously until her lower shirt was soaked. The initial zeal she had when storming off faded into a monotonous walk back to her room, where she gathered her clothes and took a long, hot shower instead.

Upon returning to the bed she had long dreamed about, she looked up in horror at Soojimu relaxing in the exposed rafters, patiently awaiting her arrival.

"So…" Soojimu said. "How was your trip?"

The pain in Kiko's stomach returned as she searched for potential lies to tell when asked about the gift he requested before their departure.

"I'm tired, Soojimu. Can you come back tomorrow?"

Soojimu's thick unibrow furrowed. "Why are you tired? The moon has only begun to rise. Unless…"

"Unless what?"

"Unless you forgot to bring back what I am owed."

Annoyed, Kiko blurted, "First of all, you asked for a gift. I never said I didn't get it. But you shouldn't expect people to give you things all the time. I don't owe you anything! Ever!"

"Is that how you feel? I only came to see how your trip went. It was you who was so unkind as to try and kick me out because you were unable to fulfill your promise."

"And how do you know?"

"Why, I heard you ask your grandmother for something, of course. I only assumed it meant you forgot about your dear friend, Soojimu."

Kiko's head dropped to her chest in shame.

"I did forget. I am sorry. I didn't intentionally forget, but I got hurt. Really bad. And everything got so crazy after that, it just slipped my mind."

"What happened?" he asked, grinning widely.

"I am honestly so tired. I cannot begin to explain."

"Well, consider your story my gift in that case," he insisted.

"Really? That's it?"

"Of course. Nobody said the gift had to have material value."

So Kiko sat up on her futon, ignoring its warm invitation to sleep, and told Soojimu all about their recent adventures. He was the best audience, sitting at the edge of his seat as she talked about the manifestation of her ancestors, chattering his teeth when she spoke of running away and nearly drowning in the river, clapping in anticipation of the magic Tomi used to heal her, and "oohing" and "aahing" at the anamorphic transformation of the Yamamayaa and riding manta rays.

Kiko decided not to tell him about the caves they visited. For some reason or another, it appeared the information was not pertinent for Soojimu, so she moved right passed that and began discussing the Iron Dragon, which caused him to wince with pain.

"What's wrong?" Kiko asked.

"It's nothing. He's very dangerous. Very dangerous. You know, I am actually feeling rather tired myself," Soojimu added, faking a long, drawn-out yawn.

"Can I ask one more question before you leave?"

"It will have to wait. I must leave. Bad fish, maybe," Soojimu said, rubbing his belly.

"Wait, I thought you said you were tired?"

"Yes. Tired and upset stomach!" he declared, painfully faking one ailment after another as he backed out of the room and into the garden.

Kiko watched him jump several feet into the thick banyan trees and disappear within its branches.

"He's not telling me something," Kiko whispered to herself and rushed to her bookbag, grabbing a pen and scribbling "Cafe - Iron Dragon Research" on her hand before lying back down for a much-deserved rest.

Kiko's dreams were a vibrant re-telling of their last few days, mixed with rich mythological themes from La'akea's mo'olelo. She dreamed of Kama'pua'a chasing her in the forest and Soojimu coming to her rescue, only to be eaten by the voracious pig deity. Another of the girls relaxing at the waterfall with Tutu and La'akea before a large dragon leaped from its cascades and attacked them, but when Kiko opened her mouth to combat him, her teeth began to fall out, leaving everyone to perish from her hesitation.

The last dream was the worst, perhaps, because it felt the most real. She was swimming in the open water, and a hundred-foot dragon made up of metal scales, a steel-toothed spine and red, volcanic eyes grabbed her feet, pulling her under. She kicked and screamed, then kicked some more, but to no avail.

She watched, outside herself, as her mother dove into the water and fought off the beast. She saw herself kicking her mother's head and shoulders, trying to make it back to the surface and finally, the jaws of the dragon clenching around her waist and dragging her to the seafloor while Kiko made her escape.

"Mom!" Kiko shouted, now awake, crying and hyperventilating with cold sweats.

Tomi's feet hustled across the tatami mats before she flew the door open and rushed to Kiko's side. She held her and rocked her gently, chanting underneath her breath until Kiko began to breathe calmly.

"I... I saw. I saw him... He... He killed her! I knew I felt her when I... I..."

"Akisamiyoo," Tomi replied. "Don't speak. It's okay. Come, let's eat."

They helped one another up and went to the kitchen together. Tomi prepared some cool hibiscus tea and searched her cabinets for goodies. Letting out a small breath of excitement, she revealed an assortment of confections she had been gifted with, and they reveled in it, eating up all the mochi, shortbread cookies, and azuki bean pastries, arranged artfully on the platter.

"How come you never make this kind of stuff for us?" Kiko asked jokingly.

Chuckling, Tomi responded, "So bad this food. All sugar, no benefit. Junk. Sometimes, it is nice. But you girls, always with your junk food. So Amerikaa."

"Amerikaa?"

"Amerikaa. White people. They love their bad food. It's no wonder they die so quickly," laughed Tomi.

Kiko offered a half-smile, half-frown look at Tomi before joining in on her laughter.

After all, Kiko was used to people poking fun at her hapa blood or "haafu," as Kyoshi said, but it struck a particularly painful chord with her when Tomi made fun of it too. She couldn't help being half-half, nor could she escape it, especially here. At least in Hawai'i, nearly everyone is hapa-something. But even then, being half-Okinawan meant you were only half as hairy, half as dark, or half-as anything. Being hapa meant you couldn't be completely a part of one culture or another because you were always met with some kind of half-ass argument as to why you didn't belong.

But for now, Kiko found peace in Tomi's company. She hadn't spent much alone time with Tomi since Yuki was always attached to her hip. So instead of pressing her buttons asking questions about the past, Kiko decided to ask something about the future instead. "What are we doing tomorrow? Or today I mean?"

"Hmm. We are preparing for Obon season for the next short while. You may not enjoy it so much, as I will need you home to study and practice alongside me. I know you like your time in town, but you will need to stay home to learn."

A look of guilt rushed over Kiko's face.

"Kachan, I need to tell you something. I know you'll be angry but…" Kiko said, "I made friends with a kijimunaa. I know you and Yamamayaa don't like them. But anyways, Soojimu was in my room and—"

"Your room?" Tomi asked, with a single brow raised, "What did he want?"

"Well see, before we left, he asked me to bring him something. But I didn't have anything when we came back because well… everything that happened. Anyway, he told me he would take my story instead. So, I told him about our journey—"

"What about it?" demanded Tomi.

"Well that's the thing. I told him everything. Well, nearly everything. I told him about Yamamayaa, the ray ride, the cave, but… I didn't tell him about becoming a yuta. I almost couldn't. Like something stopped me from saying it."

"Because it was not meant for him to know. Your ancestors protected you from making a grave mistake."

"I am so sorry. I know I keep messing up. I just… When I told him about the dragon, he took off. He lied and said he was tired, and his stomach hurt. But I knew he was faking; I could feel it in my bones."

"See," added Tomi, waving her finger at Kiko. "Because you are a yuta. You feel instead of see. No need eyes to know what people think. We hear what they do not say."

Everything began to make sense to Kiko. She realized she had always had a certain ability to feel, sense, hear, or know what people were thinking. For years, her mother had said it was because Kiko was empathetic, a characteristic lauded by her Buddhist practice, but now she wondered how much of her life was hidden by her mother and why.

Kiko looked up, lost in her thoughts, when she realized Tomi was still talking about the dragon. "After he slew most of the kijimunaa, only Soojimu and one or two others survived. One left for Hawai'i with many of the other refugees and was never seen again. The other died in a forest fire we had many years ago. Soojimu is all that's left of his kind."

"So that's why he's so scared of the Iron Dragon?"

"Yes. It is also why he and Yamamayaa never spoke to each other again."

Shoot, Kiko thought. She had hoped to learn why they felt such a fierce loathing towards one another, and because she spaced-out for a moment, she missed a pivotal part of the story. If she asked Tomi to repeat it, she'd know Kiko wasn't listening. Instead she asked, "What would it take for them to be friends again?"

"Weren't you listening? It has been almost one-hundred years since they've spoken, and it will be hundreds of years more before they forgive each other. They may die first!" Tomi laughed, disrupting some of the tension in the air.

"I see," sighed Kiko. "But you're not mad that I'm friends with him? Or that I told him about our trip?"

"No! You did a good job to let him know what he needed to know. The dragon killed almost his whole family. He deserves to know. I am sure you remind him of his daughter, just like Kyoshi's great-grandfather reminded him of his son. He always came around trying to play with your mom too—but she was very wise."

"What do you mean?" Kiko asked plainly. "What did she do?"

"Well, for one, she never let the kijimunaa into her room. They are like those... Uhh…" Tomi said, using her fingers to mimic long penetrating fangs.

"Vampire? He's a vampire?"

"No, no," corrected Tomi. "But like one. Once they are invited inside, they will always come and go when they please. I put out octopus by the doors, hoping to keep him out. Very naughty for him to be inside. He knows better. Better you make the rules. They are tricky characters, Kiko-chan. They like to bend words and manipulate even the closest of 'friends.'"

Kiko thought long and hard about what Tomi said, but she was overwhelmed with absolute exhaustion and relief and expressed it with a loud, powerful yawn.

"Here, eat this," Tomi said, handing over a small clump of black sugar. "For sweet dreams."

Once Kiko returned to her room, she laid awake, going over

everything in her mind and sleeplessly created new scenarios in which she said something with greater wit or more bearing, acting braver than she really had been. But each time she returned to an unexplained aching sensation that riddled her body, mind, and spirit.

She hadn't considered why Soojimu only wanted to be her friend, and not Yuki's, or ever thought to ask if he ever had children of his own for that matter. I guess after hundreds of years, it would only make sense that they had kids too. Kiko wished she had paid better attention to Tomi when she told his story.

As she peeked over her shoulder, she saw the rays of the sun beginning to hug the top half of the sooji screen and knew instantly that her fate, much like day and night, was already determined—it was up to her to embrace it.

The Obon Festival
(Kiko)

Days passed into weeks while I focused on learning various prayers, chants, and guidelines to empower myself as a yuta. Yuki became engrossed in her own studies and spending time with Kyoshi. He was at our house nearly every day to play, eat, or teach Yuki to play sanshin. He was a skilled musician in all things Okinawan. His grandparents loved to show off his new teeku drum and hapi, as he practiced and prepared for his eventual performance at the Obon festival. I felt a little jealous watching Yuki and Kyoshi have so much fun showing off their bon dance moves, while I tirelessly practiced making teas, setting up altars, and attempting to communicate with our ancestors.

To celebrate the season of harvest, Kachan ceaselessly worked on my "elocution" of ancient Ryukyuan rites and rituals and enunciating Uchinaaguchi words clearly, as to not confuse ushii with ushiin and "covering" the sun instead of "unveiling" the lunar cycle by mistake, which I had already done several times. In Okinawa, the yuta communicates thanks and gratitude to our ancestors, so they may inform the gods, who bless our people with continually good harvests and fishing.

Therefore, it was imperative that I learned everything from hand gestures and depth of bowing to how to move my mouth so it's a higher or lower pitch to appease the spirits. I was pretty impressed by how much I was learning, despite how bad I normally was at "education." Being a yuta meant using all the stuff I was already good at, like carving things and working with plants. But it also meant putting on really stiff clothes and letting Kachan attack my hair with a brush, as if it could be tamed in this kind of humidity. Since Uchinaaguchi didn't require reading, I got better at understanding different words and started picking it up faster in conversation.

Yuki and I would use it to talk smack about haoles who passed by our house, taking pictures of us in the garden (like we were some kind of tourist attraction) before Kachan would smack us for saying bad words, yet smiling when we said them anyway! Kachan was a real piece of work, and I don't think I will ever figure her out. I didn't even know if she slept herself. I mean how could you get any sleep with thousand-year-old ancestors bugging you all the time? From how she made it seem, it was pretty miserable to be caught up in generations of traumas and grievances. It reminded me of that one scene from Mulan, where all the ancestors are in the prayer room bickering at each other, but instead of being able to leave, they followed her wherever she went. I swear, she only sings so she can tune out their voices sometimes.

Speaking of spirits, I hadn't seen Soojimu since that night he left. I wondered where he had been now and then, and if he was okay. Honestly, I was so busy, it was hard to keep up. But every night, I left him a little bit of food outside, and if we didn't have leftovers, I poured him a small glass of the awamori that Kachan hid under the sink instead. Every morning, the dish or glass was cleaned, so it was either him or one of Yuki's shiisaa who got to it. I hadn't met either, but I figured as I got better at this yuta business, I would be able to see them eventually the way Kachan does.

She told me that the dogs age with their owners, which would make Kachan's dogs ancient, I suppose. As they age, they only get larger. In fact, Kachan told me that even though I couldn't see them yet, they overshadowed the Iriomote Yamamayaa by three-fold, making them over sixty feet tall! Yuki said hers are small, no bigger than our old dog, Manapua, a blue-nosed pit bull that stood only a foot or two tall.

I sort of missed Yuki while we were busy doing our own things, and so our time together wasn't as bad as it used to be. We normally stayed up, laughing or telling stories about what we had done, or learned, or saw that day. She helped me with my Uchinaaguchi, and I helped her learn about, well, everything I was learning. I couldn't understand why Tomi wouldn't include her, but I figured it was an age thing, and she didn't want Yuki distracting me from our practice.

As the days for Obon grew nearer, more villagers came and went from our house, hoping Kachan could get them in touch with their ancestors. They always left food, awamori, and other decadent treats in return. I felt pins and needles or other tingling sensations more frequently, and I heard voices with sharper precision that nobody else but Tomi could hear. Even my vision began to change because I swore I could see shadows or lights that I couldn't see before. But every time I sat down to chant and tried to manifest our ancestors, I failed.

Kachan was growing frustrated with me, scolding me more harshly with every mispronunciation. One time, she felt bad and let me go out to play for a little while, between guests, with Kyoshi and Yuki. I had to come back in the middle of our water balloon fight to sit in and watch over her like a shadow, as she executed different rituals with however many people. I felt like every time I looked outside, they were playing a different game or had left to play somewhere else.

In fact, I was getting distracted by everything I looked at. The mats were stickier than normal, and one had a stain that I wanted to clean so bad, my skin started to itch. I couldn't stop staring at it, until Kachan swatted me with her small fan to get my attention. It was really hard to remember all of this stuff without knowing all the words. I didn't want Kachan to think I was going to fail her either. But cramming this much stuff in my brain made it impossible to remember anything! I was still learning basic words and phrases, and she wanted me to memorize whole chants!

But all my frustrations seemed to melt away while I watched her help people. I could feel the energy in the room change each time someone came and left. I could read the looks on their faces and saw the hope come back to their eyes. This was going to be my future. I needed to stop making excuses and start coming up with solutions, or I was never going to get better. I would never be able to help all of these people.

Accepting the Facts

As the days progressed, Kiko remained vigilant in her studies. She took vigorous notes and began to sneak a daily coffee can in from the new drink dispenser in town, so that she could stay up and rehearse some more. Tomi would wander to and fro, trying to keep up with Yuki when Kyoshi stayed home but maintained a mindful eye on Kiko, dropping off snacks and drinks as she made them. Kiko would practically inhale them each time, without breaking contact with her notes and drawings, even forgetting to thank Tomi now and then, to which Tomi would clear her throat and wait for Kiko's manners to swiftly return.

"Nifee deebiru!" exclaimed Kiko, her mouth stuffed with musubi.

Tomi waited until Kiko swallowed and said it again, politely, before leaving. However, Kiko could feel Tomi's eyes on her now and then, and it warmed her spirits with a sense of pride. With only a few breaks to use the bathroom or bathe, Kiko would be holed up in the prayer room or outside in the garden, focusing on herbs, words, and history.

At dinner, Kiko found it odd that Tomi called her over, as lately she had grown accustomed to simply being given whatever meal Tomi created, as to not disrupt her learning.

"This came for you," Tomi said, handing over an envelope and a package.

Kiko frowned as she read the envelope, written in her father's handwriting. She remembered it from the last letter they'd received from him. Instead of opening the letter, she decided to open the weathered flat-rate box decorated with red hibiscus, "Aloha," and "forward to" stamped next to crossed-out other addresses from "Tutu," and in the FROM section signed, "You Know Wea." Kiko let out a quick laugh before turning it over and onto the table.

Out of the box poured several clear packages of candies (some melted together), li-hing mui powder, macadamia nuts covered in sea salt and green onion, bars of silky milk chocolate wrapped in mini individual packages, and a black and gold Kona coffee encasement Kiko promptly passed to Tomi.

Yuki snatched a couple of the bags and fled to the opposite side of the room, hastily opening each one and shoving as much as she could into her mouth, as though convinced Kiko or Tomi would soon take it away from her.

Tomi shared her disdain for Tutu sending so much junk food with a short, simple "bleh" and insisted that Kiko open the letter from her father, nudging toward it several times. Unlike the original letter, this was much more informal, sent in a plain but dirtied white envelope. Under the pressure of Tomi's intense gaze, Kiko sucked her dusted red fingertips, sticky from the li-hing mui goodness, and scraped her forefinger under the opening.

"Ow," yelped Kiko, shaking her hand in the air before sucking on the small paper cut.

"Heeku naa," Tomi waved on. "Yumi'agiree!"

Kiko unfolded the letter to reveal what looked like chicken scratch smudged against its faint blue lines and enlisted Yuki to read instead.

Yuki cleared her throat very loudly.

Dear Kiko and Yuki,
I hope your summer with Tomi has been fun
and this letter reaches you in time.
You girls will be returning to Naha at the end of August
to begin Term 2 in school, starting September 1st.
I've enclosed enough information and funds to cover
your travel back. Thanks to Tomi in advance.

Sincerely,
Major General Shackles
Semper Fidelis

Kiko felt repulsed. "But we can't go back! We have Obon! I have been preparing for weeks! I just started getting better at all of this. I hate him. I hate him so much!"

"I know!" Yuki shouted. "Me and Kyoshi have been practicing our dance non-stop! What am I going to tell him?" she asked, stomping her feet.

"It's okay," cooed Tomi, comforting the girls with her soft and supportive tone, counting the money inside the letter. "He included too much—how about we have lots of fun?" she said, fanning herself with the money jokingly.

Pocketing the yen, Tomi excused herself to go to her prayer room, where she chanted, while the girls sullenly devoured their hordes of candy. When Kiko stood up to throw away the box, she noticed a bright pink envelope stuck to the inside. "Holy Buddha, I'm glad I didn't throw this away," she said and handed it to Yuki. She opened the envelope and read its contents aloud.

Aloha babes,
I hope you girls stay enjoying your time wit your ohana dem.
What you guys wen' forget us? No call, no nothing.
No ack, ah – for I fly ova dea and lick you guys! Ha!
Jus kidding, Bebeh. Tutu misses you both very much.
The new family downstairs very niele and never like give
me da mangos from my own tree – ău-wē!
Speakin of haoles, ya faddah wen tol' me you guys stay on
one odda island. Donkey nevah like give me da address so
I hope you girls get these goodies before dey go rotten.
Try send me one lettah wit ya new address, ah? That way I can check
in more often. Eh! Why you get no number fo' call?
What kine backwards ass place you guys stay?
I worried bout you girls, you know.
So, write back yeah? And be sure to not mop
all da candy in one day or you gon' palu all ova – I talkin' to you, Yuki!
Okay, gotta go.
Hope to hear from you two soon.

Love yous,
Tutu

Yuki laughed wildly when she read over her name and mimicked Tutu's large movements and gestures, repeating some of the letter and poking fun at Tutu's pidgin and commentary. Kiko roared with laughter, waved her finger in a "nu-uh" fashion, and said, "I stay talkin' to you, Yuki! No ack!" She stuck out her chest and stomach to mock Tutu's.

After their laughter settled, Kiko looked over the letter and smiled before asking Yuki, "Are you ready to move in with Dad?"

Yuki sighed. "I dunno. I guess. I really like it here. But even Kyoshi has to move back. Do you think we will live close to him?"

"Maybe. His mom teaches at one of the schools there, I think. Maybe we will go to the same school!" Kiko said.

"I hope so! Did you see Kachan's stink eye when I read Dad's letter?"

"Yeah, I think she's really mad. I mean, we've been getting everything ready to celebrate here. If you ask me, he deserves a swift kick to his boto."

"Dollar!" Yuki shouted. "Whoa—you owe me like fifty bucks by now!"

"Whatever. But I'm serious. He just thinks because he's our dad, he can pick us up and drop us off wherever and whenever he wants!"

"Um, well yeah. He's our dad."

"Barely! For what? A few months? We barely know him! We've known Kachan longer."

"So? He's still our dad. Who knows, maybe there will be a festival there too! At least Kachan gets to take us. We don't have to go by ourselves, like last time," Yuki added, as if this would bring Kiko comfort.

"Never mind! You don't get it, Yuki."

"Hey! Are there any more watermelon candies left?" Yuki asked.

"Seriously? That's what you care about? Whatever. But no, there isn't," Kiko said with an sinister grin, her hand shoving down the remaining watermelon candies a bit further into her pocket.

"That's okay. I'll just take these," Yuki said, grabbing another plastic package of Crack Seed snacks. "Welp! I'm gonna start packing!" She said and hurried out of the room.

Kiko walked over to the buchidan room, where she heard Tomi actively chanting and quietly whispered, "Kachan? Chikee neeyabiran ga yaa?"

"Kiko-chan, iimisooree," invited Tomi.

"Nuu soo ga?" Kiko asked, watching Tomi pray over her altar, bountiful with various foods, drinks, and what looked like yen, but a Monopoly version.

"I am getting everything ready for our departure to Naha. I must make sure our ancestors have what they need here first," replied Tomi, as she used a thick brush to paint black marks over the thin, red, oblong paper lanterns.

"Kuree nuu yaibiiga? Wait, am I saying that right?"

"Jootoo, excellent. This is our family's symbol. I paint it on the chochin lantern so that our ancestors can find it in the night and guide them here: home. We do this on the first day, unkee for 'mukae-bon,' invitation. Very important. You never did this with your anmaa?" Tomi sighed. "Akisamiyoo, maybe baby time, Sako-chan was always very happy to hang these lanterns up!"

"We had something like that in Hawai'i. But they normally float them in the sea," Kiko said.

"That's naichi style. Not Okinawan. Very different. But in today's age, people like that style," Tomi said sternly. "Even though the lanterns hurt our water ukami. Gumi."

Kiko was used to hearing this. Every Okinawan she knew made it very clear that "there's a difference" between all things Japanese and Okinawan. Tomi, especially, always found a way to boast about Okinawan culture, history, and art.

"What's gumi?" Kiko asked. "I don't remember that word."

Tomi responded, "Trash, litter."

"Right, I never thought about what happens after they float out to sea. I bet turtles and stuff choke on them, thinking its food."

"Yes, very harmful. Japanese only care about fancy-fancy things. They never think about consequences. Amerikaa, same-same. But Uchinaanchu always remembers the kami and keep them safe."

"I'm sorry we have to leave," Kiko said. "I know you were looking forward to celebrating Obon here."

Tomi chuckled. "Ah, Kiko-chan, we have ancestors everywhere. As long as we honor the spirits, it doesn't matter where we are. I have lots of dushinchaa in Naha, even moai when I lived there long time. I was very popular, you know?"

Kiko grinned. "Oh, were you now? What's dushinchaa and moai? And wait, we can still do the ritual there then? I was worried all of our practice was for nothing."

"Nothing?" Tomi said, shocked. "You think I teach you nothing? Everything you do has purpose. Have you learned nothing?"

"No no, I didn't mean it like that. It's just, I have been rehearsing over and over so that it's perfect, and I feel like our dad... He just ruins everything!"

"Without your father, you would not be here. In my home. In this universe. You must be thankful for both of your parents," Tomi reminded Kiko, whose head hung low in embarrassment.

"I know. My mom used to say that too. She said we were lucky because she didn't even know her dad." Kiko paused. "No offense."

"I am not offended! Her dad was... very difficult person. War changed him so much. War and survival brought us together, and ironically, peace tore us apart." Tomi sighed.

"What happened? If you don't mind me asking."

"A curious mind is a sign of genius, you know? But sometimes... what is the saying? 'Curiosity killed the cat.' Understand?" Tomi said coyly.

"I'm sorry. I just never heard about grandpa. Is he alive? Dead?"

"I don't know. Maybe dead, maybe alive. He was very vengeful, you know? His hatred made him angry. His anger made him very violent with me and our children, so we left. We came back here to stay and never saw him again. In fact, it's how I came to have a moai too. A group of friends. We get together every month, and each of us give little bit of money in a pot and give to someone. Take turns one by one, so nobody has to ask and nobody has to struggle."

"Ever? What about your kids? He never tried to see them either? Wait. What?"

"No. Back then, children was woman's job, not man's. Plus, I had good business. I bought my bento shop, which you still enjoy. Sometimes we struggled, because you know, seven children is very expensive. Sometimes we were hungry or didn't have clothes. But I would trade my services for food, clothing, and tuition to survive. He was very wealthy, so some of my children were very angry with me for many years because we lived in poverty from time to time. You will find out. But we were very lucky for my dushinchaa. They help watch babies, so I can work. We help with money, so we can all eat. We did okay." Tomi smiled, taking a long, exhausting exhale before sitting down.

"What do you mean I'll find out? Find out what? And wait—you own that shop? How come you're never there?"

"I retire already! Too hot! Besides, my good friend's son likes to cook, so why not?" Tomi said nonchalantly. "Now let's see. Your aunties and uncles live on the main island. My eldest, Kayo, has nice restaurant in Naha, very popular. Makoto married Miss Okinawa, very pretty. They live in Chatan-cho. Kikue has big family too, so you will meet cousins your age. Seumi lives in my old home, in Naha, still single," Tomi added, shaking her head in disappointment. "But of course you know, Tomoko and Sako moved to Hawai'i a long time ago."

"That's only six," Kiko stated.

"I know. My youngest, Kyoshi, died last year. Cancer. Too much smoke cigarettes."

"Oh, I'm so sorry," apologized Kiko.

"It's okay. We speak often. He is very happy in the spiritual realm. You will see," Tomi said calmly.

"Wait, so I've been meaning to ask... How come I haven't seen my mom since that day we were in the caves at Iriomote?"

"Ah, because you have not cleansed your soul of guilt. We cannot see those who we have tied to the earth with our worldly desires. Before you can see her, you must first become at peace with your past. Wakain?"

"I understand. But that means if I can become at peace with our past, I can see her, right? Because I was hoping that during Obon..."

"Aht!" Tomi interrupted. "You are not ready to see her, Kiko-chan. It is very difficult to summon the ancestors. It took me many years to be able to call on any one individual. You are only learning simple things, like an apprentice, you know?"

"I know! I do! I just... I figured maybe we could see her. Maybe if I could just talk to her, I could get answers and maybe—"

"No!" Tomi's tone sharpened. "Do not rush. It makes you sloppy. Slow is smooth, smooth is fast. You will learn with time."

"But how am I supposed to be at peace if I can't just say sorry? Why won't you just let us see her?" Kiko shouted impulsively, before cowering under Tomi's flared nostrils and raised brows.

"You see!" Tomi's tsk'd, her tongue flickering like a snake. "You are filled with anger, Kiko! Until you discover its root, you will never find peace. How will you believe your mother forgives you if you have not forgiven yourself?"

Kiko fell to her knees in tears before Tomi even finished her question. There was no doubt that Kiko woke up and fell asleep to feelings of shame and guilt, regardless of whether or not she enjoyed her day. Tomi was right, because until Soojimu's spell, Kiko was wrought with memories of her mother, and they always ended with watching her sink below Kiko, in her attempts to save her daughter. She went to sleep every night with the look of her mother's face before she disappeared, afraid but resilient, everything that Kiko wanted to be.

"Wassaibiin, Kachan."

"Aht! Aht!" Tomi asserted. "Guburii sabitan, you mean. One is 'I'm sorry, excuse me.' The other means 'I am sorry.' Don't forget."

"Right, I confused the two. Sorry," Kiko apologized, wiping the tears from her face and sniffing as the tears subsided.

Tomi smiled. "It's okay! You learning so well! 'Miinai chichi nai', you know, we learn by watching and listening."

"I really like learning from you. Back home the teachers scold me or the kids make fun of me because it takes me longer to read or do stuff. But here, it feels so... So…"

"Natural," Tomi suggested.

"Yes! Natural like there's pressure, but there isn't. I feel like some of these words I've been saying my whole life! Like obaa or anmaa when I called Mom, but people always said I was speaking Korean or something!"

"Your language is the root of your culture, Kiko. You must never forget. Always water your roots, or they will inevitably die. Anyway, you should go pack. Don't forget to let Soojimu know you are leaving. Kijimunaa can become very jealous, you know?"

"I will. Wait. What do we do for kijimunaa on Obon? Is there anything I should make for him?"

Tomi grinned. "Yes, just make the food you normally make for him. Give him extra awamori though. Use the one in the back. Taste better."

Kiko's jaw dropped. "But how did you—"

"I notice everything. Besides, your ancestors gossip. That's how I knew about Soojimu. You took your great uncle's favorite awamori to give to him. He was very upset."

Kiko's could feel her heartbeat in her throat. "I'm so sorry, I didn't think you'd notice."

"You didn't think I would see." Tomi laughed, pointing at her milky eyes. "As long as you don't waste, eto shinjichi nu ada nayumi—kindness is never wasted."

This brought a great deal of warmth and relief to Kiko, who thought she might be punished.

"Thank you, Kachan. Well, I'm going to go back and stuff. Do you mind if I make his offering in the kitchen?"

"I already said you could, didn't I? Listen, Kiko-chan," scolded Tomi, shaking her head in judgment.

"And uh... Can you tell my great uncle I will replace his awamori? I'll do extra chores to save up. I'm really sorry," Kiko said, looking around as if trying to apologize to a happenstance spirit wandering around.

A warm draft filled the room, and Kiko knew that he, whatever his name was, accepted her offer and apology. Kiko looked forward to learning all about their ancestors, their names, history, loves, and regrets. The feeling alone was enough to remind Kiko to press on, if for no other reason than to fill her deepest void: a sense of belonging to something bigger than herself—a family she could be proud of.

Sometimes the "Crazy Family" Is Yours (Kiko)

Leaving Kachan's was difficult. Our last few days were spent cleaning the house like crazy, visiting tons of people so Kachan could bless and cleanse their homes, and finally packing and saying our goodbyes. It turned out Kyoshi wouldn't be going to school with us, since his mom thought we would be going to school on base. Which really sucked because it was like we had to start over, all over again.

But we were lucky enough to go back to Naha together, since he had to get ready for school as well. His mom offered to take us school shopping. She knows "where to get the best deals and cheapest uniforms," but Kachan insisted she would handle it because we had to go on a "field trip" first. At least, I think that's what she said. I was excited for one thing—precious internet access and strong wi-fi, so I could find anything and everything about Okinawan history, language, and yutas.

Kachan made fun of me for thinking I'd find any good information on the internet, claiming that no real yuta would trust such sacred information to the public, and anything I read would be "history as told by the enemy." It was funny hearing her complain more and more about Japanese and Americans as we got ready to leave, but then she would talk about all the places she couldn't wait to see. She was a walking conundrum, and I loved it.

Kachan was a little four-foot-something bundle of chaos the morning we had to leave. Her silver, wavy hair was frizzed up and poufy, like a bad hair day. And without a bra, her shirt exposed her long, saggy breasts, which she laughingly wrapped around her waist, telling Yuki it was a belt.

I couldn't tell what was going on, but I could feel the excitement, nervousness, and a number of other feelings in the air. Honestly, it was making me queasy. Which must have meant I was getting better at manifesting the channels and energy I needed to connect with our ancestors, right? Whether Kachan believed it or not, I was going to contact my mom. I had been watching her like a hawk and practicing chants and incantations like clockwork and despite sleeplessness, I was getting better by the day.

My only worry was that I still hadn't seen Soojimu since our last talk. I was worried I had scared him off because he hadn't eaten the food or drank the good awamori I'd left out lately. But Kyoshi said his family's offerings had been taken and returned with "fish in tenfold," so I was confused. I was honestly sad that we wouldn't be able to say goodbye to each other, seeing as he was my first real friend on Taketomi.

I wrote him a note to let him know where we were going and left it with Kyoshi to give in their family's evening offerings, so I was hoping he'd come around, but he never showed up. Even while we were in the water buffalo cart, I looked for him in the trees, but nothing.

It was comforting to see Tomi as uneasy as I was boarding the ferry. Since everyone thought she was blind—and let's be honest, Kachan was milking it for sure—we got to sit in the best seats in the cool air conditioning, get on and off first, and even got free headsets to listen to the tour guide talk about the islands and their history! I was pretty impressed so I paid close attention to these things that would have bored me outta my mind before.

Jeez, Kiko, I thought. You're a freakin' nerd now!

I couldn't believe how happy I was thinking that. I never thought in a million years I would be excited to be a nerd, but seriously, this was the coolest stuff ever. I have been doing actual magic! Between my mom and Kachan, I basically knew how to set a bone, heal wounds, exorcise a demon by way of the elements, and conjure up ghosts, son! Whaaaaaaaaa? I mean, sure, I may only have been able to heal cuts and summon like half of my ancestors, and it was mostly all the wrong body parts—but still, who else is doing that?

Not that brat, Maile Kawai! And you know what Kawai means in Okinawan? Substitute! You my substitute, number two! You doo-doo!

I must have said something aloud, or what I thought was a quiet laugh was really loud, because suddenly it felt like all eyes were on me and Yuki's snickering only confirmed my fears.

"Who's doo-doo?" squealed Yuki, barely containing her laughter.

How much did I say? Oh my god. Oh mah god. Omergod. It's coo. It's coo. Just look down, Kiko—you're good. There's like not even that long left. We're fine. It's all fine.

Let's just say it took time before I could settle back into my skin. Yeah, we were definitely not close, and yes people can talk for a pretty long time about disrespectful children, American kids, and "this generation lacking structure and discipline." But even if I couldn't understand their language, I could tell by the atmosphere, people were judging me left to right and front to back. The only eyes I didn't see were Kyoshi's and Yuki's, who looked only at each other, then down to the ground. We were all looking at the ground in a matter of seconds.

But the literal cringes in my skin came from the burning sensation only ice can bring, as Tomi's glacial eyes penetrated my entire spirit.

So, to do nothing else but be invisible for the rest of the trip, I spent most of my time watching the honeymooners, the sleeping tourists (who were way too comfortable with their temporary neighbors), selfie sticks going up and down like whack-a-moles, and the parents who looked like they were done with their trip. I would be too: their kids were terrible, and I was ashamed to be lumped in with them.

I was so happy to finally get back on land after what felt like eternity on the boat. Something about the consequences of doing anything stupid makes time go slower, and I wanted to fast forward to anything else.

It was great having our bags taken for us like we were special and, because we got to leave first, we didn't have to worry about being run over by people flooding into the small railway toward wherever they were going. But I didn't see my dad. Or any of his buddies. In fact, I was pretty sure he forgot about us because eventually, Kyoshi's mom offered to rent a car and drop us off. She and Kachan argued over who was going to pay, and Kachan appeared to concede, then she stuffed some money in Kyoshi's mom's purse when she wasn't looking. Kyoshi saw, and Kachan put a finger to her mouth, looking directly at him. I couldn't help but laugh because he looked so scared.

I forgot how busy it was until we were driving again. It was funny to see Kyoshi's mom weave in and out of traffic while verbally arranging plans with Kachan. Despite her stiffness and judgy looks, she had this really cool vibe, like she was back in her element. It really rubbed off on Kyoshi, who pointed out every attraction as we drove by, followed by some historical fact his mom or Kachan pointed out. Yuki was in and out of sleep the whole time until we stopped for bentos at a little hole-in-the-wall shop, and then we continued driving for another couple hours.

We finally arrived at the feet of two large shiisaa dogs, which held up the columns of the *Lion's Mansion*, a red-brick apartment building, towering over the street and overlooking the bay. After we stretched our bodies and unloaded our luggage, Kyoshi and his mother quickly departed for their journey home. Okay, so it wasn't a mansion as in "mansion." *Mansion,* as in, that's the name. I couldn't help but feel a little disappointed. I was really looking forward to having a huge house to ourselves. Instead, karma slapped us in the face, cramming us into a small elevator, and forcing us to take several trips to get our stuff to Kachan's floor.

I noticed, most of all, the smell as the steel doors opened to her front door. It smelt like jasmine, incense, and cigarettes. A tall, portly Okinawan woman with crazed salt-and-pepper hair in sweat shorts and a sweater opened the door. Yuki, as always, ran right up and hugged her, and I could tell the lady felt really awkward as she let us in, commenting to Tomi that we looked "so much like their mother, especially Yuki." It turned out that this was our aunt, Seumi, who looked after this house while Kachan was away—and not too well at that. She was messy and disorganized, with cats and other animals popping out and walking all over her things.

The kitchen, which looked unused aside from storage, was somehow terribly busy and wildly inactive all at the same time. Unlike Tomi's house, the bathroom and shower were in different rooms, and the shower room was tight, only tall enough to crouch in front of the mirror and sit comfortably in the bathing area to wash off.

But outside was where the true beauty was. Past the hanging laundry and smoggy clouds, you could see the entire city and the ocean. I could see people blocking off the roads and setting up booths for the Obon festival. Excitement tingled throughout my body.

Tomorrow, we'd go see Shuri Castle, take a tour through the old city, and grab our offerings from Kokusai Dori, which sounded pretty awesome according to Kyoshi. I couldn't help but wonder when we were going to get started with all the preparations with the festival happening the next day, but I didn't want to bug Kachan about it just yet.

When I went inside, she, Yuki, and Aunt Seumi were cleaning the buchidan room with such ferocity I figured it best to just jump in and join them, helping to "feng shui" the house in time for the festivities. I forgot until now that she was a mom too. I mean obviously, she was our grandma, but I never saw her like this before.

They couldn't seem to get along at all, but randomly laughed at and with each other. It was crazy. Then one by one, our aunts and uncles came through the house, quickly introducing themselves, and took over a room, in which they started to clean or cook or complain, then laugh in pairs at one another. At first, it was uncomfortable but something about it all tickled my funny bone; it was all just so bizarre.

"We are in a looney bin, and Kachan is our master." I giggled along with Yuki at the madness of it all.

"I know. Isn't it perfect?" she snickered back.

And something about this wild, crazy bunch just felt right. These were our people. We were finally home, where we belonged.

Awakening the Spirits (Kiko)

You know in the movies when the church bells ring, and those choir people sing something creepy but beautiful as the hero reveals some kind of mystical, powerful relic of sorts? Or walks toward their untimely death? Yeah, well that was basically me walking into this day, which was probably the most intense, craziest roller coaster of emotion I've ever experienced in such a short time—which says a lot.

The day started rough because, with so many people crowded in the house, I was overwhelmed with an energy I still have trouble putting a finger on. Leaving was chaotic because of all the roadblocks, and something else about Kachan's cool and calm attitude was irritating. I felt like we had so much to do, and we were just taking our time, chillin' amongst the honking horns and bumper-to-bumper traffic, while everyone was speed-talking over each other.

Turns out, this actually happens so often that there is a word specifically for it: "abiisuubu."

It perfectly describes our family's approach to basic conversation. What seemed really cool and together the night before, unraveled faster than loosely spooled wool between the paws of a kitten. To be expected, it eventually went dead silent, and everyone looked out of their assigned windows. Well, all except me, since I sat between Uncle Makoto and Yuki. I watched everyone looking out of their windows and listened to them mutter complaints under their breath—talk about awkward.

Since it took so long to get to some places, we either rushed through them or skipped them altogether. Then, as we walked, everyone was taking up Kachan's attention, talking about this or that, so I felt bad even thinking to ask for the tour she talked about earlier. Our only cousins, Katsu and Hiromi, were our age but other than that, we didn't have much in common. If we did, I wouldn't know because they were buried in their phones the entire time. I couldn't help but wonder if that's what we looked like back home, and it kinda made me feel bad for our mom and especially Kachan. Like braddah, she's ancient. We may not have much time left with her, and you're on your phone?

Meanwhile, Yuki and I talked in Uchinaaguchi as often as we could, which seemed to be a secret language because nobody but Kachan and Seumi knew what we were saying. My cousins made fun of us for speaking it, but it was clear by the looks on their faces they were jealous. And why wouldn't they be? I was proud of how far we'd come. Without our cell phones to distract us, we learned a ton of stuff, things we may have never learned about otherwise.

Since the fire, Shuri Castle has been closed for renovations. All we could really see were huge pitched-up construction tents and men of all ages in brightly colored hard hats working beyond the large stone walls. When I closed my eyes, I could see a roaring flame consume it whole. I could hear people screaming and crying out for help. It was deeply disturbing, and honestly, I was hoping we could just skip everything and get ready for the opening ceremonies.

Finally, we ended up in Kokusai Dori, a huge marketplace that looked a bit like Times Square, with all the moving ads and bright colors. Tomi told us how different it was from the swampy terrain she knew as a child and how American it had all become since then. I guess not many locals came here anymore, and it's just a place for teenagers or foreigners—which sounded a lot like how Waikiki was for us in Hawai'i.

But my favorite part was not the huge billboards or all of the fast-food chains we knew and loved growing up. No, it was seeing Heiwa Dori and the old market just a block or so away, hidden inside a huge warehouse-looking building. Inside was booming with small booths and stores, with the owners usually being older aunties who were talking to each other, laughing and gossiping in this Uchinaaguchi-Japanese fusion or "Uchinaaguchi Champuruu," as Kachan called it.

From there, we grabbed cantaloupe, melons, bananas, and other fruit which cost nearly 10,000 yen each! I couldn't believe the prices!

Back home, the fruit is probably the cheapest because it grows all over the island, whereas milk costs almost $10, so "we were lucky to be lactose intolerant," Mom said. I didn't know why we were grabbing so much either because I wasn't really sure how Kachan made her money nowadays, especially this much of it. But it wasn't my business, so I just did my best to enjoy the scenery and keep track of Yuki, who was constantly begging Kachan for toys or McDonald's. When we bought the last of the fish and a huge pig face, I noticed how full my arms were with goods and how empty Yuki's and our cousins' were.

"Do you want to help?" I said, leaning into them.

The boys only looked up from their phones, shrugged, and went back to whatever it was they were doing, and Yuki finally caught the hint and decided to help carry the huge pig head as if it were a headdress or something. I thought Japanese boys were supposed to be super helpful. What is wrong with them? Like seriously. I didn't get why they didn't like us so much or why their parents wouldn't insist on their help, but they were busy on their phones too, so what point was there in caring?

Meanwhile, I looked up and realized Kachan was gone. I couldn't believe that in the ten seconds I wasn't paying attention, she'd totally disappeared.

"Where is Kachan?" I asked Uncle Makoto and Aunt Kikue, who couldn't care less about my question and looked at me curiously before returning back to their own conversation.

My heart started to race and suddenly, all the people crowding into this walkway made me feel like a packaged sardine or one of those dead fish on ice we saw earlier. I just wanted to get out, I wanted to breathe. I could smell cigarettes waft through the air and knew that an exit was near. I swore I heard Kachan's laughter, so Yuki and I maneuvered through the crowds to get closer to it, nearly dropping our groceries several times, only to find it wasn't her. Instead, it was a small, Okinawan woman with a blue bingata-style bandana, smoking a long, thin cigarette and drinking what appeared to be a beer but with a small snake inside.

Yuki beat me to the punch by asking her if she had seen Kachan, describing her by her white hair and hajichi. It was only then that the woman recognized who we were talking about and pointed us in the direction of a small market nearby called Yaitaimura. I looked back to see if our family was still visible and did my best to wave them over but honestly, my arms were tired from all the bags, so we decided to keep moving forward. They'll find us if they want to, I thought.

Yaitai looked a lot like that one food village in *Spirited Away*. You know, in the beginning, except it was full of people, not pigs. Well, that is still up for debate because people were slurping their noodles loudly, burying their faces in all kinds of different foods, and yet somehow, they still managed to look at their phones or smoke on their vapes or cigarettes between bites. As gross as it was, something was comforting about being among so many people.

After scanning each lane for Kachan, we finally found her outside of a soba shop, talking stories with an older guy who wore a dark blue Yukata-style top and matching shorts. His arms and legs were hairy, but not nearly as much as his thick, bushy eyebrows, which seemed to take up most of his face. I couldn't help but feel a little angry to see her just having the time of her life, while we were panting and heaving with all the things she'd just bought, and it must have come over me because I suddenly heard myself shouting, "Kachan!"

I knew I messed up with my tone because Yuki's eyebrow raised, nearly touching her hairline, before gasping like I was in trouble. It must have been because she saw Kachan's facial reaction, which was muted in the scariest way, her blank and stormy eyes pierced my skin.

"Akisamiyoo," she said with a sigh, laughing with her friend and pointing to us.

They came over and took the bags, while Yuki happily handed over the impossibly heavy pig head to the shop owner, who brought us inside.

I hated how our sudden appearance seemed to not phase them and words continued to rush out: "Kachan, why did you do that? You just left us! What if we got kidnapped? We don't even know where the rest of the family is. How are we going to find them?"

And just as the words escaped my lips, one-by-one my family filed into the hole-in-the-wall soba shop, each taking a small wooden stool and putting their things away effortlessly before shouting out their orders.

"So, we just did all that for nothing? This was always the plan to meet here? Why did nobody tell us?" I asked Yuki.

"I dunno. I just followed you. I think I heard them say we were meeting somewhere earlier," she replied casually, pouring herself a second cup of cold green tea.

"Are you freaking serious? Why didn't you say something?" I demanded.

"Well you had your panties in a bunch, so I figured it wasn't the best time to say anything." She smiled. "So chill out and eat something. You're probably just hangry."

I heard my stomach growling. I hated it when people used that stupid word but it was pretty spot-on. But I wasn't going to let them think that, so I exhaled as loudly as I could, so they knew I was still upset. When the food arrived, its smell sent me straight back to the last Okinawan Festival we went to at the Hawai'i Convention Center. Our table was crowded with soba, pig's feet soup, oxtail soup, and gooyaa champuruu. All we were missing were those sweet anda-dogs and saataa andaagii.

As I slurped down the noodles, I felt my anger slip away. My cousins looked at me like I was some disgusting oinker, but I had learned that slurping noodles was a compliment. Besides, I didn't care what they thought of me. Neither did Yuki, who was rudely grabbing bits and pieces from everyone's bowl, trying each like some Okinawan Goldilocks.

After Kachan paid the bill, the boys grabbed the groceries, as instructed by their parents, and everyone went their separate ways. We went to the Miyagi house. I was impressed by how Kachan wandered through the alleyways so gracefully and uninterrupted. People who passed by kept looking at her tattoos and whispering to each other, but that didn't seem to bother her.

Instead, she smiled at them and nodded, which probably freaked them out because they probably thought she was blind too! There was something childishly mischievous about Kachan, and it made me laugh. She was like her own brand of rebellious superhero, wrapped up in a thinly woven yukata, dressed in tattoos and making smart-aleck remarks. I couldn't understand why mom never talked about her because she was the coolest person on the planet.

After we passed the marketplaces and crowds of people saving spaces on the sidewalk to watch the night's festivities, we finally got the tour we—I—wanted. Kachan told us about all the different spirits she wrestled with over the years, the ghosts that haunted various alleyways and hunted after vulnerable humans, and the main event, Obon.

Kachan pointed to the people outside cleaning and bringing in food from their cars. "You see, tonight is Unkee, first night of Obon. Like shiimii season we must go to our family tombs and clean the site. Then we will leave our ancestors something to drink, money to spend, prayers to remember them by, and food keep them full—most important."

"Wait, this is for them? Do they actually eat it?" Yuki asked with great curiosity.

"Yes. Kind of like spiritual fruit." Kachan laughed. "We eat, and they eat too, together as a family. You will see."

"What about those?" I asked, pointing at the bits of papers hanging off the trees.

"Those are wishes for the ancestors written by their families, Tanabata. We can do that too. Except, you are lucky because I can tell them for you." Kachan winked.

Eventually, we made it to the nearest rail entry point and walked up the long set of stairs before we waited to go aboard. I didn't understand why we didn't just take the car back, but I appreciated having this alone time with Kachan again. Even if it was just in silence. I tried to remember the sites Kyoshi had been talking about as the rail sped past them but forgot a lot of the details.

"Are Kyoshi and his mom coming too?" I asked, embarrassed I had forgotten about him.

"Yes, they will join us for the festival after they gather with their own families. Now, try to rest your eyes for a little while, Kiko-chan," she responded.

I couldn't believe how tired I actually was until then, my arms and legs sore from lugging around the groceries earlier. Right then, my eyelids got heavier and heavier, almost impossible to keep open, and I woke up to a jerking motion of the other passengers pressing on me at the full stop the train made.

Struggling to make it out before the doorways closed, I was caught off guard by how sticky and wet it was outside the cool air-conditioned subway. Yuki looked miserable. I could tell, by the look on her face, that a tantrum was on its way, and there was nothing to stop it. She sluggishly made her way down the steps, huffing and puffing to the very last one and repeatedly nagging, "Are we almost there?"

I wanted to cry out too, seeing as I was the one carrying everything else, but I could tell Kachan was getting annoyed and didn't want to add to it. After what felt like forever we arrived at the cemetery, which was crowded with people. Kachan grabbed a small bucket of water from the well and a wooden bamboo ladle thing and handed it to Yuki, who began to cry out in pain from "the weight." I grabbed it from her, just to shut her up, and we walked for about another quarter-mile before coming upon a large turtle-shaped tomb, where I stood dead in my tracks and laid everything down.

This place looked like an ancient burial ground for kings and queens, but it felt personal too, like it called out to me.

Kachan smiled and said, "We're here."

I felt warm all over, knowing that I instinctively knew this was it. Even without meditation, chanting, or prayers, my heart told me our family was here. I wasn't sure if it was because Yuki was tired or Kachan was proud, but she told me to clean the site how we discussed on Taketomi, and she and Yuki would return later. I felt confused at the sudden independence but ready for the job. I asked the neighboring grave's family if I could borrow their broom and without question, they gave it to me.

I swept up the leaves, some of which had a crunch that made me want to jump on them, but I didn't. Then I used water from the bucket and, with the ladle, gently wet the tomb, using my hand to wash away any slimy residue that distracted from its allure. I poured the leftover water over the ground and used the broom to brush away the dust I couldn't get earlier. When I returned the broom, I couldn't help but notice how happy the family was, playing the sanshin, singing songs, eating mochi, and other sweets. They thanked me, which I thought was weird since I was the one borrowing their stuff, but I just said "nifee deebiru" or "kafuushi," bowed, and went on my way.

Kachan returned with a much happier Yuki, whose hand was drenched with shaved-ice syrups, and passed me a bowl of it's a mostly-melted twin. She looked impressed with the job I had done and knelt down in front of the tomb, removing a single stick of incense, lit it, and began to pray. I insisted Yuki and I eat outside the main altar area because I had just spent so much time cleaning it. We waited for a couple of minutes before Kachan stood up and waved us on with a *rikka* gesture to leave.

"Wait, we're not staying? Everyone else is staying," I asked, confused why I may have spent all this time cleaning for nothing.

"Everyone is different. We cannot all go the same time. The spirits would become too busy. We will come tomorrow, nakanuhi, second day

—less busy," said Kachan. "Now we return to Miyagi house. But see, now it's nice and clean for tomorrow, and you will be too."

It made sense. I guess I wouldn't want to eat lunch with some stinky kid either. The sugar rush got Yuki and I through the rest of the walk until we stood outside the gates of what looked like her home in Taketomi, where two large shiisaa stood on either side of a table that said "Miyagi Residence" in thick Kanji block letters. We could smell a thousand aromas wafting out of the windows and could see several heads bobbing up and down through the sooji screens, and over the wall, made larger by their candle-lit shadows.

We removed our shoes, bowed, and were led inside by Kachan, who seemed to bring silence and awe into each room we passed through.

Family, friends, and friends-of-friends seemed to gather at Tomi's presence and cling to her aura in every space. I felt bad for her; I couldn't tell if she knew how selfish and fake they were being, but I knew, and it made me wonder if all they cared about was her ability to talk to the dead. Constantly, I felt nagging feelings of envy, spite, and desperation in my core. But with some, mostly her older friends and children, there was the same awe and appreciation that I felt when I looked at her.

I couldn't really explain how it felt because it made me cringe to think about it too deeply. I couldn't find any room I liked because I felt random tensions between people or the chaos that came from people trying to place more and more food on the already-overcrowded table beneath the family altar. It was spilling over with grapes and sweet potato vines, which leaned against the few bottles of awamori and sake, fish cakes, fried ikura, mochi, rice, and sushi arrangements—plus the hundreds of dollars worth of fruit we bought earlier. In the center of the chaos was the fat, aged aguu chiburu, whose face was larger than mine. On either side of the altar stood tall shoots of sugar cane, bamboo, and a jade sooji divider with large, beautiful red fans and golden borders.

This definitely felt like a sacred offering room. I couldn't tell if it was the smoke flowing from the incense, the steam foaming from the freshly stirred stew brewing in the kitchen, or maybe the huge pig face staring back at me. Out of the corner of my eye, I noticed a small, hunched-over lady—who looked older than Kachan—praying right behind me. Her hands had similar tattoos, except they had different shapes.

Instead of a large circle on the top sides of her hands, she had squares and lots of symbols that looked like something Yuki could draw. Instead of arrows, she had thin little lines going down her fingers and had thick stripes that wrapped around her wrists and forearms.

She was like Kachan 2.0 or something. Her energy felt unlike anyone else's in the house. It was totally calm and unbothered. She chanted so low, it practically sounded like she was humming, not praying. But whatever she was saying, it was clear she was dedicated because, even as I stood up and moved around, she didn't look up. Like some creeper, I just lurked in the room, watching her and enjoying the atmosphere she created. So much so, I hardly noticed other random people coming in and out of the room. Only when Kachan sat down beside her did she look up, with this almost childlike expression on her face, and leaned her cheek against Kachan's shoulder, taking a break from her chanting.

They talked and I listened, doing my best to translate the soft Uchinaaguchi spoken between them in my head. Kachan was telling her about us, how our mom died, and how we were living with her until we move here with our dad. I half expected her to look at me with the same pitiful expression everyone had when they found out our mom died, but she didn't. She just turned her head to the side, half-smiling, half-frowning with this weird understanding that she knew what we were going through. I felt my whole body relax, and she invited me to chant with them, correcting me from time to time, and commenting on my good posture and how my American accent needs to be "left behind." I knew what she meant and tried to laugh it off, but she didn't seem to find me very amusing and went back to talking to Kachan, ignoring me completely.

"Ummm, I'm going to find Yuki, okay?" I told Kachan, who cleared her throat loudly. "Nn…nji chaabira," I responded, in near-perfect Uchinaaguchi pitch and tone.

She grinned and nodded her head, as if granting me permission to leave, and I went off to find Yuki. She and our cousins, who barely spoke earlier, were now all playing outside with sparklers and lighting other small fireworks together. I ran over to join them, but a large banging sound stopped me in my tracks. I turned around to look toward the street and saw a large crowd of people gather around the oncoming drummers, who beat their teekus and odaiko drums in unison.

"It's happening!" Yuki squealed, as we rushed over to the edge of the property and climbed the stone gate to get a better view.

Men were holding up large paper lanterns in black and red yukatas with folded red head-wraps. Following them were men in the same clothes but with black and white striped leg wraps, holding up huge odaiko drums. Then, following them were boys and girls dressed in black with yellow and purple vests and matching purple bandanas. Behind them were girls and elders, alternating in wear from simple farmer clothes and hapis to fine, silk Ryusou kimonos, paired with equally stunning hanagasa hats, which made them look like floating cherry blossoms along the busy street. Even though each came in and out with different songs, they didn't clash at all.

With each passing group, Kachan pointed out their meaning. The drummers wake up the gods, demons, and ancestors. The lanterns guide the spirits in and let them know where to go. The dancers and songs help to entertain them, and the chondaraa entertainers help to reel in the mischievous spirits who like to hang out in the crowds or pull pranks on the audience. So that's why they always come up to us! I always wondered why the lineup was always the same. I figured it was to make sure everyone was included and kill time on stage, not as part of some ancestral rite to wake the freakin' gods!

"Rikka!" Kachan called out by the gate, inviting us to come along.

We hurried over to join her, and she held me back as Yuki and the gang rushed to the street to see the huge shiisaa dogs dancing and fake biting all the kids.

"Take a deep breath, Kiko-chan. As you breathe, I want you to focus on all the things I've taught you. Think about clarity. Think about silence. Then, think about your mother. Feel your ancestors, their spirit and once-existing bodies," she whispered.

At first, I closed my eyes and heard her chanting something. But then, suddenly, I heard nothing but a light ringing noise that felt like static in my ears. The backs of my eyelids were black, and projected onto them were the faces I saw on the boat, in the cave, in my mind, and my spirit. I saw my mother, whose face, surrounded by water, haunted me, and I winced.

"Kiko, go back to center. Focus. Breathe," Kachan continued, as I drew longer and slower breaths. "Good, now open your eyes."

When I looked up, the world as I knew it no longer existed. Instead, there was a whirring existence of people and spirits. Ghosts of all periods, aged by their shades of indigo blue, were following people, photo-bombing selfies and dancing on the rooftops and in the streets alongside the audience. Women in old, regal kimonos sat with perfect and proper form, makeup, and kanpuu buns above the performers. They gossiped behind fans and giggled amongst themselves. I couldn't even believe what I was seeing.

"Holy crap!" I proclaimed. "Kachan, do you see this?"

She smiled wide enough for her puffy cheeks to close her eyes, pulled me to her side, and whispered, "Yes. Now, give me a dollar."

After a moment of seriousness, we burst out laughing and walked down to join the others in what was the best night of my life.

Groveling at the Graves

It was difficult for the girls to wake up, and they felt as though last night's events had been nothing more than a dream. Still full and bloated from all of the late-night snacks their friends and family had bought from vendors on their way home, they struggled to roll off their small futon mats and get moving. Yuki moaned and groaned, stretching every limb, while Kiko drew long, dry blinks at the eye-watering, fluorescent lighting.

"What time is it?" Kiko grumbled, rubbing her eyes awake.

"Time to wake up," Yuki replied, remarkably awake all of a sudden. "We gotta go to the tombs today, remember?"

Of course! How could Kiko forget? She spent over an hour cleaning there the day before. The news was enough to energize her sleepy bones and get her through her morning routine. The clothes Seumi bought for the girls last night were laid out on tatami mats. Although Kiko normally hated dresses, she didn't hate how she looked in this particular one. The small bow-tied straps hugged her shoulders nicely, and the light, white, and floral fabric helped to allow what little breeze existed to breathe through. Yuki's dress was of similar style but in a bright and dramatic pink that Kiko wouldn't have been caught dead wearing.

Before leaving, Kiko was sure to change out the water bowl Tomi left out the night before, so the ancestors could clean their feet before they came inside. Then she left small offerings of grass, for the demons, and rice for passersby who may be accompanying their ancestors. Excited to show off the good job she did the day before, Kiko walked a bit quicker to the site than the others, carrying a bag of fruit and a couple trays of omusubi and sushi platters.

Her heart fell to her stomach when she saw the crypt, which was now littered with leaves and dust from the same roaring gusts of wind that had brought her and the others so much joy last night. Her shoulders sank toward the ground, and she kicked some leaves into a small pile to put the food on.

"Don't put the food on the dirty ground!" Aunt Seumi shouted.

Kiko jumped back.

Aunt Seumi sighed. "Akisamiyoo," she said, aggressively picking up the food Yuki was already reaching for and shooing her away.

Tomi, who always seemed prepared for moments like these, retrieved a small bamboo broom from her roll-away basket of goods and handed it to Kiko.

"Fortunately, you cleaned so well yesterday, we only need to sweep away the leaves." She smiled at Kiko, who looked as though she were about to cry. Kiko's eyes softened in response to the praise she received instead. "It is a sign they had a good time last night! Don't you think?" Tomi chuckled, nudging her playfully.

It was in this instance that Tomi and Kiko's mother couldn't be more alike. Kiko found great comfort in the likeness of Tomi's calm and soothing voice to her mother's. She bowed in thanks, received the broom from Tomi, and began to gently sweep away the leaves, doing her best to ignore her impatient aunt and Yuki, who was goofing off, making silly faces, and mocking their aunt's gestures from behind her.

When Kiko was finished, the family could almost see their reflections in the shiny and polished marble all around them. Kiko wiped down the engravings with a soft cloth, feeling proud that the family could see how hard she had worked.

Uncle Makoto and his wife laid out a thick, Hawaiian quilt across the site, and everyone took a seat and placed the offerings of fruit, sugarcane, water, azuki beans, rice, and mochi in front of the memorial tablets.

Everyone then prayed while Tomi approached the front of the tomb and began to chant. The family followed in unison behind her. This was the first time Kiko had heard her family speak Uchinaaguchi. Since her cousins weren't particularly good at following along, Kiko was able to relax, knowing she wouldn't be alone if she needed to take a break or check back on a word now and then, as they moved at an incredible pace.

They spent hours exchanging their favorite stories of those who had passed and listened with fascination as Tomi told tales of old Okinawa, while Aunt Seumi translated in Japanese for the kids. Tomi's tales seemed to be infinite and otherworldly; they included demons, ghosts, and demi-gods, all of whom held a part in the family's fate and fortune — and could be held accountable for generational curses too. But it was the tale of the Roo dragon and shiisaa that put Kiko on the edge of her seat. The twins got up and wrestled, acting out the roles of the two key players as Tomi continued to tell the story. Kiko watched intently, growing more apprehensive as the strong "shiisaa" pretended to grab a large boulder and throw it on top of the dragon, causing him to retreat. Their cousin "died" rather impressively, considering he wasn't childlike in any sense of the word and only seemed animated in the telling of this specific tale, which made everyone but Kiko laugh.

"Life is cause and effect," Aunt Seumi translated in both English and Japanese. Tomi pointed at all of the children and grandchildren alike before tapping her forehead. Aunt Seumi looked back at the children and said, "Always think before you act," nodding in agreement and sitting down quietly. The moment following was a reflective one, but it wasn't long before they were back to storytelling and bickering about this or that with one another. Kiko could faintly hear some members of the family apologizing to the large tomb, which she remembered was normal according to modern-day customs. Many people did this, Tomi said, because they forget about the ancestors, so the second day is used to grovel at the graves and offer gifts and good meals, praying for forgiveness.

As the sun drew nearer to the horizon, one-by-one, the large group whittled down to just Tomi and the girls, who enjoyed the sunset together.

"How come the boys don't get to do this stuff?" Kiko asked Tomi.

"They are busy. Everyone has their own life, Kiko-chan," she kindly replied.

"No, I mean like the yuta stuff. Is it only us? Or can they see them too?"

"Before, men not so much. They were busy too. War, farming, you know. Always so impatient," Tomi said, pressing her finger at Kiko's heart. "If you do not embrace our ancestors completely, you will eventually forget them. It is a full-time commitment, and laziness always begins small, you know? It starts with not lighting the incense every day or not offering food and drink. Then forgetting to pray or consult the ancestors before making decisions. Always busy-busy your generation, you know? Now days, everyone is always on their phones. Always drama. They only care about themselves. If you only care about you, how can you care for others? So, with this, they lose the connection. Never forget where you come from. If you forget your ancestors, you spit on the life they sacrificed to give you, the one you take for granted."

"Whoa, whoa! Why are you yelling at us? We didn't even do anything."

"I am not yelling," Tomi said plainly. "I am telling the truth."

They sat in silence for a bit before Yuki nonchalantly added, "Well, I, for one, am pretty thankful that our phones broke. Did you see how they were all hunched over like that? They looked like zombies. Thank god we didn't look like that, right?"

"You did, too. Just because you are not using one now doesn't make you better than them. You were just the same, I'm sure, with your mom. She was also lazy when it came to her duties." Tomi huffed and seemed to be growing increasingly upset.

"Did we do something wrong? Are you mad at us or something?" Kiko asked softly.

"I'm just tired. Busy day. Too many people. Too much noise. Too much complaining." She sighed deeply.

Only then could they see how exhausted she was. The bags under her eyes seemed to be puffier than usual, and her face was losing color, looking as pale as death once the dark night sky came slipping in.

"Okay, let's go," Tomi said, packing up the last of their things in the cart.

"Kiko, you carry this, okay? Yuki, you take the rest."

"Where are we going?" Kiko asked. "I thought we were going to see our— "

"No," Tomi said. "We need to rest. We will come back tomorrow."

The walk home was unlike any other. Despite people still parading the streets, there was a ringing sense of silence that wrapped around the group like a bubble, separating their realities. Inside the bubble, there was a stirring tension that hushed the girls while Tomi sang folk songs in a strained and weary voice. Kiko wanted desperately to ask more about the dragon and shiisaa tale but found there was no opportunity to bring it up, and even if there was, she wasn't looking forward to the foreseeable lecture about her destiny to defeat her own dragon.

Outside of the bubble, there was a bustling noise among brigades of performers, participants, and onlookers as Tomi and the girls weaved through the tide of human traffic and back to their eerily quiet and dimly-lit Miyagi house.

As they removed their slippers and walked inside, a chill ran down Kiko's back. Yuki's hand reached into the darkness to find Kiko's, which was already wet with sweat.

"Why won't she turn on the lights?" Yuki whispered in a scared voice.

"I don't know. Just shut up," hissed Kiko. "Just go to our room and turn on the light in there."

Tomi called them into the altar room, which was now bare aside from a couple plants on the tootoomee itself, where she then instructed Kiko to pray. Hesitant and almost afraid, Kiko took shaky breaths to calm herself before lifting the small, tightly-bound mallet and holding it above the bell. Tomi cleared her throat.

"You are forgetting the incense," she reminded Kiko.

"Oh right. Of course. Duh," Kiko said, searching for a lighter on the ground.

"You can light it with your mind. Just think heat. Focus," demanded Tomi.

Kiko closed her eyes and focused on fire, imagining the heat of a flame. When she opened her eyes, the incense was lit.

"What? For real? Brah! You see that?" Kiko squealed in excitement.

Tomi flicked her lighter aflame before Yuki let out a laugh so loud it shook the walls.

"Come on, Kiko, you are a yuta — not a magician. You must always be prepared," Tomi reminded Kiko, who looked a bit disappointed to have not lit it with her mind.

"Now tell me," began Tomi. "What is the difference between hinukan and tootoomee?"

"Umm... The hinukan is where we honor our gods of nature and invite them into our home to protect us... And the tootoomee is where we worship our ancestors."

Tomi tilted her head and leaned in impatiently, as if expecting more.

"And..." Kiko started, looking around for the right answer. "And where they can heal from our prayers."

"Jootoo. Why are they separated?" Tomi asked, pointing at the altars.

"Because they have different energy and require different levels of respect," Kiko answered assuredly. "Each takes root in us. But energy comes from the gods, who give it to nature, who gave it to our ancestors, who gave it to us. So, that's why their tier is highest, our ancestor's tier is in the middle, and we are at the bottom. Because that shows them we respect and honor them. Right?"

Tomi only smiled in response, the way all mentors do when a pupil thrives under pressure. Freshly humbled, Kiko scanned the tootoomee and realized it was missing water, the candle's wax was low, and the floor was still dusted with the remains of food from earlier.

So she laid the incense in its burner and excused herself to grab the broom. Then she swept the floor in front of the altars and wiped them down with a fresh rag from the kitchen. Yuki offered to help, but Kiko refused, telling her "it's my job" and continued cleaning. After filling up the water cup and rice bowl, she returned to the kitchen to wash her face, hands, and rinse out her mouth. This was a practice Tomi was very particular about to reclaim "purity" and "respect the spiritual guests."

Upon her return, Tomi gestured Kiko to sit in front of them at the altar, and Kiko diligently obeyed her unspoken instruction. Doing her best to clear her mind, she sat confidently with her legs folded on the floor, lit a second stick of incense, and finally rang the bell to awaken the ancestors. Kiko rubbed her small palms together, as if she were coming up with a plan of attack, and chanted with great tenacity and reverence, just as she had diligently practiced on Taketomi weeks before. Every time her mind fell astray, or she began to worry about "missing something," she prayed louder, her voice soon bellowing over the once tranquil room. As she did, painful and joyful memories of her mother began to stir. Small flashes of the excruciating incident started to exhaust her of breath, as she remembered the image of her mother's hand sinking further and further away from the water's surface. Tears fell from her eyes, but Kiko began to pray faster, more eloquent and precise than before. As more memories of their travels, their father, Tomi, and Iriomote rushed to her mind, Kiko found herself always returning back to the memory of the open water and the drowning, replaying over and over again.

Crying out in pain and trying to chant over her sobbing, Kiko's body began to visibly vibrate and shake against the tatami mats. First, the whole floor began to shake and then the whole room. Tomi, who held a cowering Yuki close, prayed alongside Kiko, and watched in careful observation. Kiko's breathing became faster and faster, the hairs all over her body stood up as if electrified, and when Kiko opened her eyes, they glowed with an intoxicating hue of blue and white light.

Tomi stood transfixed by Kiko's electrifying gaze, her own eyes glowing, before a light shot from their eyes to one another. Their heads shot back, and a thunderclap echoed from their lips as lighting lit up the sky outside. Kiko's meditative body lifted into the air, convulsed uncontrollably, and then slammed jarringly back into the tatami mat.

Yuki screamed, staring at Kiko's limp, cold body, and Tomi rushed to console her. "Shh. Just wait," Tomi said, restraining Yuki from reaching out to Kiko. "Utichiki. She is traveling to the spiritual realm. If you wake her body before her spirit arrives, she may not return! Now leave, or remain quiet." She bent low near Kiko's face. "Kiko-chan, remember your lessons and return safely to this body. It is only when you find the answers you need, you can return. Chibariyoo," she cooed. Then Tomi pressed together her small, tattooed hands, which glowed with the same intoxicating light and began to chant with vigor, as if her voice was Kiko's lifeline to the physical world.

.

Ichishini—Between Life and Death (Kiko)

I wasn't too sure what happened. All I remember was praying and feeling like lava was rushing through my veins and seeping out of my skin. It was an out-of-body experience, watching my body from outside myself as Kachan and Yuki stood over me. I tried to call out to them, but they couldn't hear me. Everything moved so much slower down there.

When I looked at my hands, I saw they were the same color and hue as the spirits I'd seen before. I also felt heavier, and it took longer to look around and move the way I wanted to. Kachan was saying something, as if she knew I was here, but the words took so long to get to me, it became too difficult to understand.

I honestly didn't know what to do next, until I looked outside to see brightly-lit spirits, like mine, floating all over the city. I could see every building that had existed from every generation before us, standing in their own ghostly shapes as people floated in and out of the rooms and homes to pay their visits.

I swore I heard someone calling my name, so although it took a second to get used to floating instead of flying like I imagined ghosts do, I finally made my way out to the garden. There swayed the silhouettes of the ancestral spirits I had seen before. They appeared to be eating, with a couple playing the sanshin and singing, while others drank and watched the crowds below. It felt like a surprise party, except everyone was dead and only noticed me when I said, "Whoa."

I cringed inside. Whoa? Seriously, brah? You're so freakin' dumb. I can't believe that's all you have to say, and by the looks of it, neither can

174

they. But what was I supposed to say? Ugh! What would Kachan do? Think, Kiko. Think!

Just then, a young boy rushed toward me. I would have been excited, except he was terrifying to look at. Most of the children were. I jumped, or rather floated, back before remembering this is my family. They weren't going to hurt me. All I needed to do was tell them who I was, right?

I managed to squeeze out a small greeting, "Mensooree. Hawai'i-Taketomi-nu Kiko Shiroma yaibiin," hoping that in welcoming them home in Uchinaaguchi and letting them know who I was and where I was from, they may recognize me as one of them. I remember Kachan telling me that's how the warriors used to do it, introducing their family name first. And seeing that so many of them were wearing some form of a military ensemble or another, I figured why not?

They stared at me like I had the biggest pimple on my face, but I was sure they were mostly judging my "haafu" dialect. I heard some mention my mom, while others kept saying "Amerikaa," which I assumed meant my dad. Some agreed that I looked like Miyo, pointing at a warrior priestess in full feudal armor, but she instantly denied the comment over their laughter.

Suddenly, I didn't know how to feel about being here. This felt like one of those parties we used to go to where all the aunties pick on us about our weight, our brains, or our looks: a.k.a The Asian Shame Games.

"May the strongest survive," my mom used to say in a half-laugh, half-heartbroken kind of way.

I knew I could survive this situation. I just needed to prove to them that I belonged.

I rolled my shoulders back and stood taller than I had before. My eyebrows narrowed, and I did my best to look like the warrior yuta I knew I could be. The spirits laughed even louder, but this time they pinched my cheeks, patted my head, and crowded over me. I felt chills running through my body, except it wasn't cold. In fact, it was the most comforting feeling I had felt in my life. Like whatever I was fighting was over. Something about their presence made it impossible to hold back my tears, and for the life of me, I couldn't understand why.

"Cheesayaa, Kiko-chan! We have long waited to meet you," whispered a cool, radio-deejay-type voice from somewhere among the crowd. I looked up to see an old woman with no eyes in an all-white yukata surrounded by an equally radiant light facing me.

"Yutasarugutu unigee sabira." I bowed, truly thankful to meet them. I looked among the crowd greeting me and couldn't help but feel disappointed that my mom wasn't one of them. Was she so mad she couldn't be here? Did I not chant hard enough?

"Umm, ee-tai, anmaaya maa yaibiiga?" I asked as politely as I could, hoping they could tell me where my mom was.

"Namaa wurankutu atukara kuuwa," replied the young boy with torn-up clothes and a missing arm, whose gruesome smile made my stomach curl.

It was hard to tell what he was saying because the scars around his mouth made it hard for him to enunciate. I felt bad for looking at him so confused, like maybe he thought I was making fun of him, but I wasn't. He stopped and said "Not here. Wait," in perfect English, his only hand making a *stop* motion.

I figured he had to be from the Battle of Okinawa. His injuries were like the ones Kachan told stories about. He was around Yuki's age. My heart sank for his parents, who looked nearly the same, but they had different burns and missing limbs.

I wondered why their bodies looked like this? Does your spirit look like your body does when you die? Do we get to choose? If so, why would they choose this? No, of course they wouldn't. No mother would want to see her baby look like this. But at least they were together, even if it was like this. Right? I did my best not to flinch when they talked to me because I didn't want them to relive the embarrassment of thinking I was ashamed of them. Just then, I realized I couldn't even remember what my mom was wearing when she dove into the water. I could see her face and her hands, but for the first time, I couldn't see her clothes. I felt sick. I didn't really think about what I would say to her if I did see her. I knew it was unfair that I was getting this chance, and Yuki couldn't because she would know exactly what to say. She would have thought I was stupid for not being better prepared for this.

But it was nice to be in a place where I didn't feel anything. I didn't feel everyone's energy the way I did back home. It was so satisfying to simply enjoy their company without overthinking their emotions. I tried my hardest to look patient, but I couldn't help but peep over their heads whenever a new ancestor walked in. It was probably just because we were floating. It takes longer. That's all. She will be here. Mom would at least say hi, no matter how mad she was.

In the chaos of things, I wondered how Yuki was doing. She looked so scared before I left. I wanted to check in on her, but it felt like it would be rude to leave everyone. Still, it felt wrong to enjoy spending time with our family, singing and dancing, knowing how worried Yuki must have been.

After speaking to the first hundred or so people, I felt pretty confident that my basic Uchinaaguchi was sounding better and more fluent than before. I finally managed to relax long enough to learn the words to "Tinsagu nu Hana," which played in the streets beneath us and brought teal-colored tears down everyone's faces as they talked about the Battle of Okinawa and the significance of the balsam flowers. As they finished their bowls of pig's feet soup, squid-ink soup, gooyaa champuruu, and the many other foods floating all around them, each began to say their goodbyes — hoping to catch up with friends in different households or islands, which would take a good deal of time to travel to.

Soon enough, I was alone with Sayuri, our oldest ancestor, who stayed eerily silent beside me. I studied her quietly, noticing the tattoos that traveled up and down her arms and hands. The void where her eyes used to be made me wonder what happened to her. It made her look much colder, more monster-ish than I felt comfortable with, as she stared expressionless into the distance.

How come old Okinawans don't say anything? But then I remembered the ghost story of a yuta who foretold her own death and was buried under a bridge not too far from here. Kachan said that's why we cannot speak too loudly or make too much noise. I bet that's why. Because if history taught us anything, it was that making yourself known could get you killed, and she didn't shy away from the horrors of that reality as Mom did.

"You are here because you think you know pain and misfortune. It blocks your energy from reaching its potential," Sayuri finally spoke. Except she didn't actually say anything. Her lips never moved. I realized her voice was reverberating in my mind, as though she were speaking to me telepathically. Then she slowly turned her head toward me, like how they do in scary movies, lifted her crooked forefinger to the center of my eyebrow, and pushed my third eye like a button.

Before I could speak, I felt a pulling sensation on my face, my chest, and then my spine. I blinked, and I saw myself back home in Hawai'i in the ocean water. I looked around frantically. This was where it all began, the place where I lost her. I panicked, and my lungs felt like they were collapsing, but I was amazed with how much more vividly I could see everything than I had before. It wasn't long before pulse-like sensations started to ripple through the sea, and I could see a long, dark creature lurking below. I watched as iridescent scales moved like a snake through the open water and underneath me, encircling me like I was its prey. I was so fixated on the coiling creature that it seemed as though Mom appeared out of nowhere, diving into the water and striking the beast.

My heart pounded in my ears, as I watched myself repeat the same mistake: trying to escape to the surface as she fought it off. I couldn't just sit there and watch her die all over again. I saw the body boarder in the distance and knew time was growing short. With all my strength, I broke the energy field forcing me back, and I dove under the water. She was being dragged further and further down into the ocean. Each time she managed to kick herself out of its grip, the dragon grabbed her again, playing with her the way a lion does a mouse. I let out a shriek so long and loud, I was able to finally catch the dragon's attention.

As he made his way to me, I noticed how different he looked up close: his scales shined with the same luster as metal. Even in the distance, his fierce gaze pierced my skin like the soldiers I'd met before, cold and almost mechanical. At least now I know why it was called the Iron Dragon. Within seconds, his four razor-sharp claws clasped onto my side. I thought I would be devoured, then a large orb of light sent shockwaves through the water, causing him to retreat.

The pulling sensation began again, and I felt as though I was being yanked back and forth across the water as my world faded back to black.

When I opened my eyes, Sayuri remained firm in the place she stood before the vision overtook me.

"You saw the truth, no?" Sayuri spoke into my mind, raising her chin and brow at me. I nodded. "Now it is your destiny to face it," she added, deadpan, as her presence loomed over the altar.

I could hear Kachan and Yuki over the loud humming in my mind and knew they were trying to call me back.

"But how? How do I face the dragon?" I asked, desperately, knowing my time here was almost over.

Sayuri's mouth unhinged like a habu snake and fell to the floor, and although I was afraid at first, I felt drawn toward the perilously black abyss that appeared. I found I could unnaturally walk into it, and did. In fact, I was practically sucked into this crazy space vortex created by Sayuri, as her sharp shrills pierced the air like venomous fangs. I covered my ears as best I could to keep them from bleeding and ran deeper into the darkness.

Going back to the physical world hurt. You know when you fall down steep steps in dreams? It felt like that. Except I couldn't stop falling. I couldn't wake up. I heard their voices getting clearer, louder, and faster in pace, but I couldn't do anything. I started hyperventilating until my body was shaking so violently, it shook me awake. Instantly, I felt vomit rising in my throat. I started sweating. Then I finally threw up, exorcist-style, all over the room and all over the people within it.

"Keeti chan yaa, Kiko-chan." Kachan smiled, wiping the puke away from the corners of her eyes and mouth.

I wanted to apologize, but all I could taste was acid, and Yuki began rubbing my back, which made me feel worse with each stroke.

"She's dying, Kachan! Fix her! Heeku naa!" Yuki cried out, her piercing voice making my ears ring.

"Ee! Agimasankee," Kachan said before she waved her glowing hands over me, and the last thing I remember were her bright, stormy eyes and feeling so, so heavy in her arms.

Ukui—Saying Goodbye

Kiko awoke to the sounds of people clamoring outside her room. She rose slowly, examining her body, unsure whether she was in the spiritual or physical realm. She came to her feet and stretched, moaning in pain from a multitude of fresh bruises and long, deep-set scratches, resembling the Iron Dragon's piercing claws, that down her sides and legs.

When she peeped through the sooji screen outside, she saw it was still night. The creaking of the sliding screen must have garnered Yuki's attention, as she rushed in and hugged Kiko so tightly that she cried out in pain.

"I thought you were gonna die, Kiko!" Yuki sobbed. "Everyone has been asking where you are, and I... I... I am so sorry, Kiko! I could have killed you. I almost killed you because... Because..."

"It's okay, Yuki, I'm okay," Kiko responded calmly.

"But look at you," Yuki said, pointing to the mirror across the room.

Kiko limped over and was horrified by her appearance. Her hair was crazed and standing up in all directions. It was hard to see clear patches of skin because most of her body was covered in wounds.

"What happened?" Kiko groaned.

"I shook you... I just... I just wanted you to wake up. You weren't waking up! But then your body started shaking and you flew across the room, banging all the walls and scratching yourself all over."

"Holy shit. What?" Kiko asked, remembering the sensations she felt in the spiritual realm.

"Kachan can explain. I just... I'm glad you're okay, Kiko. I was so scared," Yuki whimpered, desperately holding onto her.

Yuki fled outside and quickly returned with someone's purse full of makeup which she feverishly applied to Kiko's face and body.

Kiko laughed painfully. "Looks like all those YouTube videos you watch did you some good, huh?"

"Voila!" Yuki proclaimed, putting a mirror up to Kiko.

Kiko's face looked nearly chalk-white, aside from the dark wing-tipped eyeliner, voluminous eyelashes, and bright pink blush, all of which made her look more like a clown. Kiko's lips pursed in disgust, but she thanked Yuki anyway.

As they walked outside, Kiko used her hands to wipe away the blush, but it didn't matter because she drew the attention of every person in the house as she walked by anyway.

Those preparing the minnuku meal for the bad and wandering spirits looked up as though they had seen a ghost. The head of the table repeatedly asked Tomi if "marines got a hold of her last night," which made Kiko confused because her dad was a marine, and she didn't know what they were trying to say. Maybe they think he beat me up or something? Kiko thought before assuring them that she fell while "sleepwalking" and laughed off their concerns and cruel remarks.

Tomi, who stood over the brewing pot on the stove, looked over at Kiko and sighed deeply in relief. Kiko slowly drew breaths of strength and limped over to the kitchen to join Tomi.

"Everyone is getting ready to leave. They're about to burn the uchikabi soon," Yuki whispered in Kiko's ear.

"The what?" Kiko asked

"The money for our ancestors, remember?"

"Right, right. Okay," Kiko said, drinking some of the tea Tomi poured for her. Tomi then led them to the tootoomee room, where the rest of the family was waiting. The twins giggled at Kiko's abhorrent makeup and blemished figure as she struggled to sit on the ground, before Tomi silenced them with a look.

Seumi and Makoto sat on either side of her, asking questions about what happened when they left, but Kiko focused on the shrine and chanted instead. A renewed energy entered the room, and the mischievous and quiet gossiping ceased, as Kiko's voice championed over theirs in steadfast concentration for the task at hand.

Scanning the offering table, which was full of sake, tea, and bundles of food paired together in the jyubako bento box, Kiko reached for the yellow bundle of hammer-stamped spirit money and released it from the confines of its white seal. Nearly shaking, she lit the incense and placed it in the burner beside the tightly bound sugarcane shoots. She bowed deeply, despite the painful exhale that escaped her lips, and continued to pray as she turned over the sushi and other bits of food to allow the ancestors to eat. The family was only allowed to eat when the incense burned half-way down, indicating the ancestors were finished with their meal.

Meanwhile, Tomi poured a bit of water over a large silver bowl and strainer on the offering table. Then, she set the uchikabi ablaze and placed it inside. The red and blue flames burned brilliantly, and the same chill from before enveloped Kiko, who shivered at the fleeting feeling of approval. Using chopsticks when the fire finally smoked out, Uncle Makoto moved the remaining offerings and ash outside to be freed to the spirit world and its leftovers given to passing spirits and yuurii.

Outside, the final eisaa performances could be heard drawing to a close, as well as the roaring applause from onlookers and locals. Family members and friends began to say their farewells, as Tomi passive-aggressively made comments about the time and how late it was, while cupping her yawns to hint at her exhaustion. Soon, the house was quiet, and so were the streets. Tomi waved at what appeared to be no one and nothing in the distance before closing all the sooji screens shut and turning on the lights around the house.

"Akisamiyoo," exhaled Tomi. "Finally, it is all done. So taxing this time of year, no? Kiko-chan, make sure you eat—lots of leftovers."

"Thank you, Kachan," Kiko said, slowly gathering herself.

"You must be so exhaust—wutatoon," Tomi said, helping Kiko up.

"Kachan, I know you're tired. But I just wanted to know what happened last night?" Kiko asked, hoping to get some clarification. "Yuki told me that I was acting crazy, as if a demon took over me."

"Why? You feel sick?" Tomi asked. "That's okay you know, when I first experience kamidaari, I felt sick too. Some even lose their mabui— their soul. But you don't look like that," she said with a far off gaze. "When one loses their mabui, they seem lifeless: no energy."

"No. I mean, yes, I still feel sick. But no, that's not what I meant. Wait—how do you get it back? I mean, let's say I did lose it. How do you get your mabui back?" Kiko followed Tomi into the kitchen.

"Well, you have to first pray," Tomi said as she fixed Kiko a plate of food. "Then retrace your steps, either here or in the spiritual world, wherever you were startled or shocked enough to lose it. You take three stones and wrap them in the clothes you lost your mabui in. This gives it weight to hold onto. Then, you call to it, like a cat, 'Mabuyaa, mabuyaa, utikuuyoo,' until it comes back," she said in a cute, playful voice.

"That's it? No spells? No charms? No magic potion?"

"Why you ask so much about spells and magic potions? You know not everything is like the movies, Kiko-chan. Before all this fancy-fancy things, real magic looks more like school. You study, you practice, you learn. The world around us is magic. It is your duty to find it."

Kiko drew silent breaths, both disappointed and embarrassed. That makes sense, she thought. Harry Potter had to study for a while to do magic too. Aang took time to bend all the elements. "Okay, I'm sorry," she said and continued eating the leftovers. She told Tomi about all the people she met and everything she saw in the spirit realm before her abrupt return. "Kachan, what happened to Yuito and his family? Why don't they look like the others? You know?"

Tomi took a long, deep breath and answered, "Ahh, Yuito-chan. He was my little brother, your great-uncle. He and my two brothers died. You probably met them. Very handsome."

Kiko cringed because most of the spirits from that era had been burned, blown up, or otherwise battered. She didn't know how handsome they could have been, but she imagined if she lost Yuki, she would forever think of her as the beautiful, wild girl she was.

"When you see them, what do they look like?" Kiko asked.

Tomi chuckled softly. "You were scared by their looks, yes? I told you, life is not like a movie. When you die, you enter the spirit world however you go. Only those lucky enough could afford to die with beauty and grace. Not everyone meets the same fate, as you saw. But maybe something to think about when we pick out our clothes, no?"

Kiko looked down at what she was wearing, and her cheeks began to burn.

"And before you ask—no," Tomi said sternly. "I don't know where your mother is or why she didn't talk to you. My only guess is that you were not ready."

"How did you know I was going to ask about my mom?"

"Kiko, it is all you talk about. Of course, I know you'll ask. By the look on your face, I know you never saw her."

"Was that before or after I threw up everywhere?" Kiko asked jokingly, taking another bite from her plate.

"Definitely before. I was not looking at your face after. I was looking at the floor I just cleaned!" Tomi laughed loudly.

Kiko joined her, finally beginning to relax. "I'm sorry I always talk about her. I know it must be annoying."

"No, painful sometimes, you know, to remember. Not annoying. If I were you, I would be like this too. But I knew already, the powers of a yuta, so when my family died, I saw them right away, some I hadn't seen for years while I was away at school. Sometimes, that's how I found out they had even died," Tomi said, pursing her lips tightly, and then encouraging Kiko to continue eating. "You must be hungry—eat everything! I remember during kamidaari time, I always had this ravenous hunger. Every day, I get sick, so I never gained weight. So skinny! Now, used to it, so gravity follows me everywhere I go," Tomi said jokingly, pointing at her stomach, arm fat, and sagging breasts.

Kiko wanted to tell Tomi all about her dream but didn't know quite how to put words together to explain the experience. Instead, she asked about what would help her plan for the "destiny" Sayuri mentioned. "So, what is kamidaari again? I don't remember you using that word before. Or maybe I hit my head so hard, I must have forgotten."

"It is time between normal life and yuta life. Sometimes it takes years, and for some people not so long—depends on your nature and shiji. Since you are young, your mind is not yet corrupted by this or that. Your imagination," Tomi said pointing at her temple, "allows you to see and feel what is already there, what many adults ignore. So as adults, some people go crazy! I remember a young woman who would hide naked in the forests because she denied her power, and it consumed her mind. Very dangerous sometimes, the ancestors can be."

"Wait. Naked? Like no clothes at all?" Kiko asked, shocked.

"Naked as the day she was born! Screaming and cursing at everyone, pulling her hair. But each day, she got closer to the Utaki, hidden deep in the forest. It was there she realized she could no longer deny her fate and accepted her role as a yuta."

"Is she still alive?"

"You met her just the other day! She was here! With the hajichi, same-same like mine."

Kiko winced. "Her? Did this happen like a long time ago?"

"Maybe thirty or forty years ago. Her kids were already grown up."

Kiko shook her head in disbelief, hardly able to imagine the old woman she met earlier jumping out of bushes naked and scaring people. She seemed so calm and collected, like Yoda or something.

"But why was she naked? That doesn't make sense. I'm not a kid, you know. You can tell me the truth!"

"She kept going to the Three-S trail, sleepwalking every night. She thought the spirits wanted her clothes. So, she took em' off! She did stuff like this all the time. People thought she was crazy: 'schizophrenic' they call it now. But this is kamidaari," Tomi said proudly, emphasizing each word with a tap of her hand.

"Did you, like, do that too? Wait, am I gonna be running around naked somewhere?"

"No! Well, maybe. I do not know. I come from long line of yuta, so we do not experience this because, like you, we are trained by someone who recognizes the signs. She did not know, so she endured tatari—punishment—for denying her calling. Some people have to suffer for a long time to activate their power, you know."

"You mentioned before that you knew right away I was going to be a yuta. How did you know?"

"Our power is unlike any other. We can always sense someone with shiji, the energy needed to speak to our ancestors. It surrounds you like a light. It is why people will naturally draw themselves to you, like moths."

Kiko remembered all the people who would come up to her, the adults who would randomly vent to her about their problems, and the power of "empathy" her mom always talked about.

"That's so crazy. Sometimes when I talk to people, I can feel everything they're feeling. But more than that, I can see their whole life almost. Especially my friends. Wait. Does that make sense? That sounds weird out loud, so maybe I'm not saying it the right way."

"No, that is part of being a yuta. We feel so much, sometimes, too much. Most people just want to talk, talk, talk to the dead. That is the most painful task, as you will experience. But most times, we can see and feel everything from everyone. Because not only we feel their spirit, we feel the spirit of all their ancestors. It is why it is very exhausting to be yuta, especially during Obon."

"Right, of course." Kiko sighed, realizing she no longer wanted to burden Tomi with her dream or questions. "I'm so sorry. I know you must be so tired. You should go to sleep, Kachan. I will clean up."

"Yes. I am going to sleep," Tomi said as she lightly tapped the edge of the table. "You need lots of rest too, Kiko-chan. But I won't stop you from cleaning. Just don't wake up Yuki. She was so grouchy all day, like a baby banshee—waa-waa-waa," Tomi mockingly wailed.

Then, as Tomi walked down the hall, she turned briefly to Kiko and said, "You know, sometimes when I think-think-think, I chant. Maybe it will make you feel better."

Kiko smiled and they bowed to one another before Tomi retired to her room. Kiko cleared the table and began to clean the dishes. She did her best to sing the off-tune folk songs she heard and mumbled through the words she didn't know while she swept the floors and cleaned off the tables.

Just then, she heard a light tapping on the sooji screen door. It sounded like rain, but there stood the large silhouette of a man with wild hair and a long, hooked staff. She rubbed her eyes and looked again, yet he remained. Her heart raced as she looked around, trying to decide whether or not she should scream, hide, or answer the door.

A Means to An End

"Kiko-chan, it's Soojimu," the figure whispered loudly. "Open the door!"

Kiko stood still. Soojimu never left Taketomi. What would he even be doing here? He was certainly not this tall either. "Prove it!" Kiko hissed back at the figure.

She recognized his bellowing laughter but listened carefully, a tooth's skin away from the sooji screen, where he lightly began to tap his long, talon-like nails.

"Let's see. Well, for one, I know you're not as foolish as to keep me waiting outside."

"Be more specific."

Soojimu chuckled. "You live with an old bat of a woman you call 'Kachan' and even met her little kitty-cat friend, no? And you forgot my gift, which I did not forget!"

Kiko let out a sigh of relief.

"Now, let me inside. This place is dangerous for those like me."

Kiko peered down the hallway and looked around the room before quietly sliding the screen door open to let him in. The lantern he carried made him appear taller than usual in the shadows, so Kiko felt relieved to know he was back down to his child-like size upon opening the screen door.

"What are you doing here? If Kachan wakes up, she'll kill us both," Kiko whispered.

"Well, I went to your house because I smelled the food you left behind, but you were gone. I waited for two days, you know! Anyway, so there I was, eating, when I saw two Amerikaa warriors in leafy clothes, snooping around. Of course, I scared them away. But they came back, twice! The second time, they almost got inside."

"Wait, what?"

"Yes, yes. Luckily, you have Soojimu to protect you! For the first time in hundreds of years, I showed my face. You should have seen them! So scared they were! Like little fish in the ocean! They scurried away quick!"

"But what did they want?" Kiko asked.

"I don't know, but I couldn't find you or your fat little friend. Then I saw you, you know. I knew you activated your power. The kami told me. All the land is talking about your shiji, you know."

"What do you mean all of the land knows?"

"Aiya! When you entered kamidaari, you automatically became one with the land. You can see all, hear all, feel all the centuries that existed, no?" Soojimu asked.

Kiko remembered seeing the towering buildings that didn't exist anymore and all the people from previous centuries. "How did you know that?" she asked, glaring at Soojimu suspiciously.

"The kami, of course! The gajumaru trees connect us all and they leaf to gossip. Get it? Like live to gossip? No? No?" Soojimu asked, looking at Kiko half-offended for not receiving any laughter in response to his pun. "Well it's okay, you no understand Soojimu's funny joke. It was a hit with the Unis. But anyway, maybe everyone who is anyone in Yaeyama knows about you now," he added.

Kiko stepped back, hesitant to ask anything else.

Soojimu cupped his palm against his lips as if he was telling a secret. "Don't worry! It's a good thing! Nature will protect you now," he encouraged. "Plus, with her on your side, nobody can harm you," he said, pointing down the hall.

"What do I tell Kachan about her house? What if they rob her while she's here! Why aren't you there to protect it?" Kiko demanded.

Soojimu tilted his head to the side, confused and upset. "Ay, I travel long time to see you, and you complain that I'm not there? I'm not your soldier to boss around! Besides, her shiisaa will never let anyone who harms her home leave with their soul intact. Shiisaa are dangerous, you know! They tear your mabui right out of your body. It's why they have such sharp teeth!"

"I'm sorry. I'm just tired. I was hoping that I could try to go back tonight," Kiko said, looking toward the tootoomee room.

"Ahhh, you mortal souls. You need so much to be happy, don't you?" Soojimu asked with a sadness Kiko hadn't heard before.

"No, I just... I never saw my mom. I really need to talk to her."

"Never? You sure?"

"I think I would know if I saw her, yeah."

"Interesting. Maybe you're not ready," Soojimu said bluntly.

"Why does everyone keep saying that? Look, thanks for your input, but you're wrong. I am ready."

"Tsk. Tsk. Tsk," clicked Soojimu. "This anger stops you from seeing them. It is my anger that stops me from seeing my family too."

Kiko was reminded that Soojimu was actually alone, and she lowered her physically defensive stance, "I'm not angry. I mean—I am, but not at her."

"I never said you were angry with her. Your problem, Kiko-chan, is that you are angry with yourself. When you forgive yourself, you will see her. In fact, she is probably waiting right now!"

"But how do I do that?" Kiko groaned.

Soojimu laughed. "You're asking me? I just told you I cannot see my own family."

"Seriously, Soojimu. You must know!" You're a thousand years old!"

"Well, you have to think about what you want. It has to be clear in your mind, without fear or doubt. You need to see your mistakes clearly and admit to them. Then you must remember you are only human, for human mistakes are the greatest tools of knowledge. If you focus on how you benefit from your mistakes, you will learn to forgive yourself."

"But what if my mistakes cost someone their life?" Kiko asked.

"Well, we both know you are not responsible for her death—right?"

"Yeah," she replied plainly. "I guess you're right."

"Well then. It should be no problem. Unless you're lying?"

"It's just... If I just... If I wasn't in the water that day. If I didn't beg to go swimming, or if I just realized the tide carried me so far away, she would still be here."

"But you were swimming. Like all kids do. You didn't know she would drown. If you knew, would you still go?"

"No, of course not!"

"Well, I am no yuta, but I can tell you right now it sounds like you didn't plan on her death. So, why would you be at fault for it?"

Kiko knew the answer. She knew it wasn't just her and her mother in the water that day. She knew the truth, but she couldn't admit it to herself or Soojimu.

"Because I wasn't strong enough to save myself. I wasn't strong enough to save... her."

Kiko began to choke up and Soojimu inched toward her. "Now, now. Don't cry. Want me to sing? Maybe that will make you feel better."

He began to sing what sounded like an ancient folk song, loud and nearly yodeling the opening notes. Kiko threw her hand over his mouth to hush him. He licked her hand, and she shook it away, repulsed by the slimy residue he left behind.

"Eww!" Kiko squealed, rubbing her hand onto her pants, sick to her stomach all over again.

"Well, next time, just ask! Don't be so rude! You know, some say I have the voice of an angel."

Kiko's stomach gurgled loudly before she emitted gas so foul, so loud, that Soojimu curled over in pain.

"Excuse me," Kiko said, thoroughly embarrassed.

"You foul beasts with your petulant bowels!" he shrieked, rushing toward the screen for fresh air.

"I'm sorry, okay! I can't control it! It's partly your fault!"

"Akisamiyoo! It's sickening is what it is! I can't bear the scent of it! Goodbye!"

Soojimu yelped, his fingers pinching his nose and his palm covering his mouth as he backed away. Then he threw open the screen door and rushed to the gajumaru trees.

"Well, that settles that," Kiko said aloud, rubbing her aching stomach. "Ugh, I wonder if she has Cheong Ro Hwan somewhere."

Kiko limped and moaned back to the kitchen, searching the cabinets as quietly as she could for the brown glass jar with the sunset-orange cap, full of magical but smelly cure-all little black balls, but with no such luck. Unfortunately, she knew of only one other remedy: the bitter concoction Tomi always kept at her side. A medicine made from pig's brain, tons of spices, and awamori. The smell alone was enough to make her sick, but people from all over the village would come to Tomi for this medicine, so she knew it had to work.

"I can't believe it's come to this," Kiko murmured to herself, as she opened the fridge door to find the small vial sitting by itself, almost ominously alone. She popped off the cork lid, pinched her nose tightly, and threw its contents to the back of her throat, trying to swallow all of its bitter intensity at once.

Almost instantly, Kiko felt her symptoms alleviate. Returning to her room, a loud gust of wind flung the shutters open and shook the entire house. "Seriously? What is it with tonight? Is nobody waking up to this, seriously?" she wondered aloud, her eyes wide and scanning the room from corner to corner.

Kiko quickened her pace, flew back into her room, and quickly took cover under the sheets.

The Last Sakura
(Kiko)

I didn't know how anyone could sleep through all that racket. I couldn't get comfortable at all! Like I swear it's took Yuki ten seconds to fall asleep, while it took me thirty-nine different sleeping positions and a sacrificial goat to get any rest. Between the streaming memories from the last few days, to Soojimu acting all crazy, to my aching body, to this ridiculous weather—it was just too much. I kept tossing and turning, seeing flashes of the Iron Dragon each time I closed my eyes. I felt like I needed to be in the altar room. As if I wouldn't be able to sleep until I gave it another go.

Aside from the wind, all I could hear as I walked through the house was the slight swishing of my feet against the tatami mats, gliding through the halls and into the room. I'm not sure how I missed it before, but for some reason, the only photo that stood out in the altar room was the sepia-toned one of my mother in her one-piece bikini and sash after winning Miss Okinawa many years ago.

I never knew that until our aunts told us. We heard people call her "Miss Okinawa" all the time, but she always insisted they were joking. She looked more beautiful than ever in this picture. I hoped maybe one day, I'd look like her too.

"I think everyone is wrong about us, you know," I said to her photograph. "They just don't understand what I am feeling. Everyone thinks I just feel guilty or sad or lost. But that isn't it at all. People don't understand the relationship we had."

I remembered when she was too tired to take care of Yuki, but I was there. And when Mom couldn't stop crying but wouldn't say what was wrong, I held her. On days Tutu couldn't help out, I was the one making our lunches, dinners, breakfasts, doing the laundry, and taking care of the house. I didn't just lose my mom. I lost my best friend too.

"You know, when I look at Yuki, I feel bad because I know she didn't have what we had. I know that we had something special. She was too young to remember all the hard stuff we had to go through together. Moving to a new country. Learning a new language. Nobody could understand that but us. So when everyone keeps saying I haven't let go, they just don't get it! I am allowed to be angry and sad. I have every right to be because I didn't ask for this! I didn't ask to live a life without you!" I cried out. "I just have so many questions. Mostly about how to help Yuki. I don't know how to do her hair or help with boys or do makeup. I just want to remember how to make poultices the way you did and all the gardening tips I ignored and recipes I never paid attention to."

I felt tears forming behind my eyelids and pushed them back with my fingers, taking a long and silent pause. I lit the incense and decided to instead focus on my breathing and chant, as Kachan told me to. I had to remember to get back to center. I had to remember to forget everything around me if I wanted to see her. But then again, I didn't want to forget. Every chant I uttered echoed back a memory because all I wanted was to remember her. I wanted Yuki to remember these things too because I worried she was already forgetting her. I didn't want the only thing I saw when I thought about Mom to be the image of her dying to save me from the Iron Dragon. I wanted her to know she didn't die in vain, that I would do whatever I could to defeat him. But more than that, I wanted her to know that even though she wasn't here, I still felt her. When I closed my eyes, I still saw her. In fact, right then, I still felt her breath and heard her voice calling out to me.

"Kiko-chan," a haunting voice echoed from above.

I looked up, staring into her raven-black eyes, as she appeared to be swimming toward me, gracefully floating in her favorite dress. Even in death, she was so beautiful. Her obsidian hair flowed like silk against the matter that enveloped her nearly mythological presence, and I was consumed by it.

Even though my eyes began to sting, I couldn't look away. I had wanted this so bad for so long, I didn't even know how to respond now that the moment was finally here. I felt stupid. I was afraid, but most of all, I was so undeniably happy.

Her voice, just as cool and heartwarming as I had remembered, seemed to softly travel through the air like smoke: "Hello, Kiko. We have so much to talk about..."

Acknowledgments

This was a huge community project and with that, there are so many people to thank. First and foremost is my mother, Sato Nakanishi-Shankles, who inspires me constantly and always made it a point to invest in our cultural upbringing and Okinawan pride. I also want to recognize our entire Nakanishi matriarchy, who have raised countless children and endured so much but always made the impossible seem possible. To my sisters, Samantha and Scarlett, who watched my daughters while I worked ceaselessly on this manuscript, studied religiously (pun, intended) and helped to keep my head up when I was struggling to finish. Let's not forget my father, Rick, whose wholesome views allowed me to become an activist against militarization, despite his military history. Of course, to my loving partner Kama, who endured my sleepless nights and blasting Okinawan folk songs "just to think right." And to my tribe: I want to thank Chris for introducing me to his daughter, Toni, who changed my world and brought my imagination to life. Lydia, my editor, whose patience and direction allowed this project to be completed to begin with. My Okinawan brothers and sisters: Brandon Ufugusuku-Ing, who introduced me to a world of Uchinaaguchi and constantly teaches me something new about our culture, people, and heritage. Lee Tonouchi, who always inspires me to be true to myself and write stories for our people. Taurie Kinoshita (Oki in spirit!), Eric Wada, Joyce Chinen, Pete Doktor, and Jeremy Keuma—my people, whose networking skills allowed me to find the people necessary to complete this work. Finally, in memory of the family members who largely inspired many of the characters but passed before they could ever see this book—we have so much to celebrate at Obon: Tomi Nakanishi (2015), Kayo Nakanishi (2017), and Kyoshi Nakanishi (2018).

Ipeei nifee deebiru

Intro to Uchinaaguchi

My mother, Sato Nakanishi-Shankles (Naha-Urasoe, Miyagi village), would first like me to explain that the Okinawan language (Uchinaaguchi) is not a "dialect" or "hōgen," as often indicated by the Japanese government. During Okinawa's annexation, the language was forbidden and frowned upon as Uchinaanchu were forced to assimilate. This has led Uchinaaguchi and Kunigami to be on UNESCO's "endangered" list.

A. Introduction:

Once the primary language of the Ryukyuan Kingdom, Uchinaaguchi has been spoken for several centuries (1400s until 1879). It has differences depending on which village or island one is visiting, such as Mainland Okinawa, Amami Island, Miyako Island, and Yaeyama Island or Yonaguni Island. Now, although Tomi is from "Taketomi" (which has a different language from Uchinaaguchi) please note that she was born in Naha and moved to Taketomi after WWII.

Recently, efforts have been made to revitalize Uchinaaguchi in Okinawa and Hawai'i—where many Okinawans (Shimanchu) fled during the Plantation Era, in hopes of a brighter future. Today, Hawai'i has one of the world's largest collections of Okinawan texts, books, and classes where the language can be enjoyed.

The writing system of Uchinaaguchi used in this book is largely based on OEW (Okinawan-English Wordbook, Sakihara 2006) which adapted the Hepburn system with the modification of long vowels and glottal sounds. The dialectal focus is primary to Shuri/Naha districts within *The Last Sakura*.

Translations were verified by Brandon A. Ufugusuku-Ing and others, who you can also support via donation to Ukwanshin Kabudan (Hawai'i Chapter).

B. Pronunciation Guides:

Pronunciation is based on OEW (Okinawan-English Wordbook, Sakihara 2006) which adapted the Hepburn system with the modification of long vowels and glottal sounds.

Vowels:
a as in sakura
e as in anime or eisaa
i as in flee
o as in Oh or Obon
u as in Ooo, that looks delicious!

Long vowels:
aa, ee, ii, oo, uu

They have the same qualities as when single, but are longer in duration and typically, e and o are found only as long vowels. In many cases one may see the (¯) symbol over a short vowel, to represent long vowel sounds.

C. Consonants:

There are nineteen consonants, p, t, k, b, d, g, s, z, j, h, f, m, n, r, w, y, sh, ch and '(glottal stop). Although rare, "z" sound is pronounced as j as in "jar." The glottal stop: " ' " is a glottal stop marker and it is pronounced like English 'uh-huh'(yes), uh-uh(no). It is often contrasted with non-glottal (smooth) sound waa (my...).

Another example is 'yaa (you) ≠ yaa (house). In general, glottal vowels precedes the vowels either y or w in word-initial position. The glottalization occurs in other environments as well. They are the sound initiating short nasal syllable n as in 'nma (over there), 'njitachi (departure), and 'nni (rice plant) ≠ nni (chest).

f : pronounce with the two lips as the point of articulation (rather than the upper lip and lower teeth of English f). as in 'knife' or 'funeral'.

g: always represents as hard g, as in English 'gift' or 'grandma'. However, if there is an 'n' preceding the 'g', the two consonants are never pronounced together i.e. 'nothing'. Instead, it is pronounced separately i.e. angwaa 'young girl' is pronounced as an-gwaa (not ang-waa).

r: represents a short flap t sound, like water splatter allover in English.

D. Fun Facts and Language Tips:

Brandon A. Ufugusuku-Ing explains that in Uchinaaguchi, there is no equivalent to "Ohayou Gozaimasu" or "Konnichiwa" (Japanese) because in old Okinawa, everyone knew each other in their villages, so there was no need for formalities unless meeting someone new or in terms of honorific use. Instead, Shimanchu merely exchanged "in the moment" commentary. Please read Brandon's commentary regarding "Ukimisoochii" below regarding language barriers between Kiko and Tomi:

"This one is confusing for people, because it is often translated directly as 'ohayou gozaimasu,' and thus taught that way. However, it actually is a question, asking, 'Have you woken up?' So technically the reply would be 'I am awake/I woke up.' i.e., 'Ukimisoochii' should not be responded to with 'ukimisoochii.'

Based on the writing so far, I take that Kiko does not really know uchinaaguchi, and Tomi is making an effort to teach Kiko that greeting. In which case it might be pretty natural that Tomi is satisfied with Kiko replying with the mirrored 'ukimisoochii,' simply as a repeat-after-me exercise.

The other thing is, because I assume Tomi is older than Kiko, Tomi wouldn't use 'ukimisoochii' because it's a formal greeting. But, again, it does feel like a teaching moment, so if Tomi is trying to model by example, it would fit.

Now, just as a suggestion, what if you added this to the conversation... so after Kiko gets 'u..kimi..soo.chii' out, Tomi has a little proud moment and says 'yasa! ukitoon doo!' So Tomi first celebrates with 'Yasa! (that's it!),' and then, maybe sort of jokingly, answers Kiko's 'ukimisoochii' with 'ukitoon doo! (yeah, I'm awake!).'"

E. Words and Expressions:

Achaa yaa	See you tomorrow
Agaa	Ouch!
Agimasankee	Don't rush me!
Ai	whoa!
Akisamiyoo	Oh my goodness (expresses shock, stress, etc.)
Ammaa/anmaa/ayaa	Mother
Chaabira sai/tai	Hello at the door before entering; I am here
Guburii sabira	Excuse me (before leaving)
Ee	(expression to get someone's attention)
Huu/Uu	Yes
Haisai/Haitai	Hello
Hajimiti wuganabira	This is our first time meeting/Nice to meet you
Hicharu haku gwaa	Shiny box thing (Soojimu).
Ikahii/Ikayii	I am leaving/Goodbye
Ichutaa matchimisoori	Please wait a little while
Iimisooree	Please come in
isujimi sooree	Please hurry
kumankai kuuw	Come here
Kuree nuu yaibiiga	What is this?
Kwatchii sabira	Thank you for the food (before eating)
Kwatchii sabitan	Thank you for the food (after eating)
Ma kai gai?	Where are you going?
Maa san/Maasan	Delicious!
Mata yaa sai/tai	See you again/See you later!
Mensore/Mensooree/ Mesooree	Welcome
Mutchi kuu	Bring that to me
Nifee deebiru/ Nifeedeebiru (Ippei Nifeedeebiru)	Thank you
Nji chaabira	Good bye; Lit. "Farewell"
Nuu sou ga?/ Nuu sooga	What are you doing?
Nibuii	Tired/Sleepy
Niibuyaa	Sleepy head

Ukimisoochii	You are up? Lit. "You are awake?"
Usagamisooree	Please help yourself (when eating).
Wassaibittan	I'm sorry (I was wrong)
Wassaibin	I'm sorry (excuse me)
Wakayabitan	I understand/ Okay.
Uumaku	Rascal or Troublemaker
Uchinaa	Okinawa
Uchinanchu/Uchinaanchu/	
Shimanchu	Okinawan People (local)
Uchinaaguchi	Okinawan language
Yi asa yaibiin yaa	It is a nice morning, yes?
Yi yuru yaibiin yaa	It is a nice evening, yes?
Yonna atchimisooree	Please walk slowly/Take it easy/ Be safe!
Yukuimisooree	Please rest/Goodnight
Yumi'agiin	Read aloud!
Yuurii	Ghosts
Yuntakuu	Talkative

F. Numbers:

1 – tiichi 2 – taachi 3 – miichi 4- yuuchi 5 ichichi 6 – muuchi
7 – nanachi 8 – yaachi 9 – kukunuchi 10 – tuu

G. Proverbs: (Provided by Okinawa.com)

Unji washiririba yaminu yunu kumichi, wadudu sukunayuru ayumigurisa. *To forget a debt of gratitude is like being on a path in the dark night, it is easy to lose oneself and, is very hard to walk through.*

Ataishi turu atairu. *We get along well with those we can get along with well.*

Ichariba choodee. *Once we meet and talk, we are brothers and sisters.*

Uya yushi kwa yushi. *Parents and children teach one another.*

Kuchi ganga naa ya yakutatan. *A smooth talker is a good-for-nothing person.*

Shikinoo chui shiihii shiru kurasuru. *Let's live helping each other in this world.*

Shinjichi nu ada nayumi. *Kindness will never be wasted in any way.*

Jin too waraaran kwa tu ru waraariiru. *We can laugh happily with our children, but not with money.*

Chu uyamee ru duu uyamee. *If you respect others, they will respect you.*

Choo kukuru ru dee ichi. *The heart is the most essential human quality.*

Tusui ya tatashina mun. Warabee shikashina mun. *The old should be treated with due respect. Children should be treated with gentleness.*

Yuu ya shititin mii ya shitinna. *Even if you hide yourself from the world, don't lose sight of your real nature.*

Nmarijima nu kutuba wasshii nee kuni n wasshiin. *Forgetting your native tongue means forgetting your native country.*

If you have enjoyed these readings please consider downloading *Rikka, Uchinaa-nkai! Okinawa Language Textbook for Beginner*s and purchasing the *Okinawan-English Wordbook.*

In addition, if you found this to be helpful and would like to continue supporting the communities that host free workshops that educate our Shimanchu communities in perpetuating Uchinaaguchi, please consider donating to the Ukwanshin Kabudan/Ryukyu Performing Arts Troupe of Hawai'i, The Center of Okinawan Studies at The University of Hawai'i at Manoa, and Hawaii United Okinawa Association (HUOA).

Ippei nifee deebiru | Mahalo nui loa | Thank you very much

Made in the USA
Monee, IL
13 February 2024

53474761R00120